SPANISH DISCO

ERICA ORLOFF

is a transplanted New Yorker who now calls South Florida home. She is a writer and editor who has worked in publishing for over a decade. She is the coauthor of two books of humor writing, and the coauthor of *The Sixty Second Commute* about the home office phenomenon, as well as two books for children, including *The Best Friends' Handbook*, aimed at empowering teen and preteen girls. As an editor and ghostwriter, she has worked behind the scenes on many publishing successes.

Erica despises the "c-word" (cooking) and likes to write on her laptop, poolside. She presides over a house of unruly pets, including a parrot who curses as avidly as she does. She loves playing poker, a game she was taught by her grandmother, and regularly enjoys trying to steal her crew of wonderful friends' money playing five-card stud.

SPANISH DISCO

Erica Orloff

RED
DRESS
I N K
™

First edition January 2003

SPANISH DISCO

A Red Dress Ink novel

ISBN 0-373-25023-1

Visit Red Dress Ink at www.reddressink.com

Printed in U.S.A.

To my parents, Walter and Maryanne Orloff.
And to the memory of Robert and Irene Cunningham.

Acknowledgments

I would like to thank my wonderful, beloved agent,
Jay Poynor, for always believing in me and my work.
You are friend, cheering section, critic, confidant, and family.

To my father, Walter Orloff. I am a writer because, first and
foremost, you are a terribly interesting character. Second, you
are the father in chapter thirteen who challenged me to read
well beyond my years. All I am is because you challenged me.

To my mother, Maryanne Orloff, who bears *no* resemblance to
the mother in the pages herein. My love of reading stems from
your love of reading. Thank you for taking me to the library in
second grade, letting me sign out seven books on a Friday and
taking me back on Monday to sign out new ones.

To my sisters, Stacey Groome and Jessica Stasinos,
and to my girlfriends, Pammie, Cleo, Nancy, Kathy L., Kathy J.,
Lisa, JoAnn and Meredith...for your friendship and support.
To Kathy Levinson, in particular, for tolerating
my trips to New York (and giving me a place to stay)
with my over-the-top fear of flying. You are my personal
"flying shrink." Thanks to Marc Levinson, as well—
same reasons. And to Pam Morrell, especially,
thanks for believing I am "winsome."

To the members of Writer's Cramp:
Pam, Gina, Becky...and Josh.

To the members of my women's book group,
for your friendship (and great food once a month).

At Red Dress Ink, thank you to Margaret O'Neill Marbury, for
your insight and wisdom and belief in this book. And to all the
people at Red Dress who made this book possible.

To Alexa, Nicholas and Isabella.
Thank you for giving me a reason to breathe.

To my godmother, Gloria, and to my cousin Joey D., because
I always promised you I would mention you in my book.

To the late Viktor Frankl. I live because of your philosophy.

To anyone I've somehow left out. You know I'm not that
organized, so please forgive me.

And finally, to J.D.
You know all my secrets, even the ones I share with no one
else, and you know all my pain and joys. And though I often
want to kill you, you make me laugh *every day*.

1

"Hello, Buttercup."

Most people panic that a jangling phone at 4:09 in the morning is a death call—the one in which a cop is about to tell you he's found your sibling or mother or father plastered like a bloody possum on the pavement of I-95. Instead, I uttered his name like a curse: "Michael!"

"Yes, darling, it's me."

I reached in vain for the lamp.

"I don't suppose there's any point in asking if you know what time it is."

"What would David have for breakfast?"

"Breakfast?"

"Because I think eggs indicates a surprising lack of concern about his health. After all, his wife has been nagging him for years about his cholesterol. His smoking. And this could be his lone act of defiance. His way of telling the world to fuck off, as you, my dear, would so eloquently put it."

"Or he could merely like sunny-side up and a side of bacon, Michael. Is it that important what your character eats for breakfast?"

My fingers found the little pull-chain on my bedside lamp. I squinted and reached for the glass of warm bourbon and water I keep on my nightstand for conversations precisely like this one.

"Vitally."

"Michael, you know I am not at my best until a good, solid six hours from now. And that only after a pot of coffee. Can't this wait?"

"Be a love," he said, his English accent trying to charm me through the phone line. "Greet the dawn with me."

"Greet the dawn? Michael, I don't want to greet the dawn with you. I don't want to greet *noon* with you."

"Impossible! You don't want to enjoy the splendor outside your balcony with me? Your favorite author?"

"*Favorite* is not—*most definitely not*—the word that comes to mind right now." I sighed. "Those acknowledgments better drip with praise."

"To my dream editor, the love of my life, Cassie Hayes, without whom this book would not be possible and without whom I would curl into a fetal position and remain there. For life without the beautiful and witty Miss Hayes would, in fact, be life not worth living at all."

"That's a start."

"And she has a remarkable sense of the sublime and a true command of all dangling participles."

"And?"

"And she's simply charming before the dawn."

Stretching, I sighed. "All right. Let me grab my robe and start a pot of coffee."

"Are you naked, Cassie?"

Michael Pearton was, quite possibly, the best writer I had ever worked with or read. He was also faintly mysterious. His back cover head shots showed a man with black curly hair and a crooked smile offset by a long, ragged scar on his decidedly square chin. He was both movie-star handsome and bar-fight dangerous. We'd never met but indulged in flirtation bordering on phone sex. Because I wasn't getting any other kind of sex, I tolerated his predawn ramblings.

"Why, yes, Michael, I am," I murmured. "Stark, raving naked. My nipples are hard because you know I keep my house colder than a meat locker regardless of what the weather is outside. And I am now shoving said nipples into my robe and shuffling in my bare feet to the kitchen where I will start a pot of coffee."

I rested the portable phone on my shoulder, talking in my pre-coffee rasp as I tied my green silk kimono, a gift from another author's trip to Singapore.

"I do so love it when you talk dirty, Cassie."

"I do so love it when you call me in the middle of the day."

"So nasty when you haven't had that cup. You know you

should switch to tea, love. Do you ever use the set I shipped you?"

I flicked on the kitchen light, shielding my eyes from the brightness as it reflected on my Florida-white tile and cabinets, and stared at the sterling tea set perched, never used, on my breakfast bar. He had bought it at a flea market of some sort and shipped it over to the States. It was tarnished, but the elaborate handle on the teapot was ornately baroque, and though it matched nothing in my condominium, I adored it.

"Yes. It's gorgeous."

"You're a horrible liar. But I know it probably looks lovely wherever you have it."

"Michael, why does inspiration only strike you in the middle of *my* night?"

My Mr. Coffee machine started making noises, and I willed it to brew faster.

"It's very odd really. I go to sleep and wake up in the middle of the night absolutely certain of what must happen next. Oh…and showers. I get inspiration in the shower. And now, everyone else in London is getting ready for lunch, and I just have to finish this scene. It's sad, really. I have a twenty-thousand-dollar antique cherrywood desk good enough for the queen herself, and I never write a damn word sitting at it."

I knew he was sitting stark, raving naked in his bed, with his laptop and a hard-on for companionship.

"So your inspiration is that David is worrying about breakfast?"

"Yes. It's the morning after he's been denied tenure. He feels completely emasculated. And now, as an act of defiance, I see him having eggs."

"Okay, then. Let him eat eggs."

"What kind?"

"Michael, who the fuck cares what kind?"

"What kind? Would he eat poached eggs or scrambled?"

"I thought I mentioned sunny-side up with a side of bacon."

"But that was an offhanded comment. I don't think you really gave it much thought."

"Poached."

"You think so, really? What about eggs Benedict? Because then he would be eating all that wicked hollandaise sauce."

"I don't care, Michael. Give him hollandaise if it makes you happy. It's four-thirty."

"Is your coffee ready yet? You certainly are particularly crabby this morning."

"Michael, I don't know a single other editor who would put up with this kind of shit."

"Precisely. Which is why you have authors eating out of the palm of your hand, and Louis O'Connor has the most successful small publishing house in the States."

Eyeing the coffeemaker with lust, I smiled. "Coffee's almost ready. I'll be human soon."

A minute or two later, I sat down at my kitchen table an ocean away from West Side Publishing's most valuable author. Michael clicked away on his keyboard, and I drank coffee and held his hand long distance as we worked through the scene. He'd been blocked. I knew he couldn't get past the fourteenth chapter. Every book was the same. Somewhere in the middle he lost hope. He gave up. He got sick of his book, its plot, of his own characters. And then he didn't work for a while until he had an epiphany— usually in the middle of *my* night—and called me and we talked for hours waiting for the sun to rise and, with it, the resolution of his crisis. Although I think it was an excuse to hear me talk about my nipples.

"Michael," I yawned two hours later, "the sun is rising."

"Tell me about it," he whispered.

I stepped out onto my balcony, facing the view a Boca Raton condo can buy. "Well, the Atlantic's really calm this morning—a beautiful azure blue. I see a seagull gliding lazily and a pelican swooping down. The sun is just peeking—the horizon is pink and purple and still midnight a little. The crescent moon is sharing the sky with the beginning of the sun. And here it comes.... God, it's beautiful, Michael."

The salty breeze kissed my face.

"You give good sunrise, Cassie."

"Well, if it weren't for you, I'd never see them, so I guess I should thank you. But I won't. I'm going back to bed."

"You've had a pot of coffee. Aren't you wired?"

"No. Good night, Michael."

"Good morning, Cassie. You are the bloody best. Thank you."

"May the next time I hear your voice be after lunch."

I hung up and ran a hand through my bedhead of messy black curls. I padded back to my room, drew the blinds tighter and dropped my robe, crawling sensuously beneath my sheets. I loved the decadence of going back to bed. I picked up the phone and dialed the office, pressing extension 303.

"Lou...it's me. Michael Pearton had another pre-dawn meltdown. We were on the phone discussing his main character's menu choices 'til just now. It's 6:30. I'm exhausted. I won't be in until at least noon if you're lucky."

I shut my eyes and thought I'd skip the whole day at the office. My boss let me work three days at home, thanks to voice mail and e-mail, and his sheer adoration of me. I was supposed to go in on Fridays, but the hell with it. I turned the ringer off on my phone. Sleep returned quickly. I dreamed of swimming in pools of hollandaise.

At 11:00, the phone rang, muffled, out in the kitchen. I could hear the caller ignoring the fact that I wasn't answering. I heard four rings, a voice speaking. Hang up. Four rings. Voice speaking. Hang up. Four rings...

"Oh for God's sake, what do you want, Lou?" I finally snatched the receiver next to my bed.

"How'd you know..."

"You're the only person stubborn enough to do that, Lou."

"I need you in here today."

"Sorry. I put in my hours with the ever-neurotic Englishman last night. Or actually, this morning, but you know what I mean. I'll be in on Monday."

"This is big."

"What do you mean?"

"Bigger than Stephen King, big. This could make me millions. Your bonus could send you into early retirement."

"So who is it?"

"Can't tell you."

"Lou...this isn't high school. Not that I think you ever went to high school. You were born eating your young."

"Cassie, my dear, you come and go out of here as the diva you are. But this one time, I'm telling you to get up, get dressed, and meet me at the office. I will mainline you a pot of coffee."

"This better be worth it."

"It is. In spades."

I climbed out of bed, still far too early for my taste. In the kitchen, I dumped out the grinds in Mr. Coffee, the only man in my condo in the last year and a half, and put on my second pot of the day. After a hot shower, a dab of crimson lipstick, and a sort of shaggy-dog shaking of my hair, I dressed in jeans and a T-shirt, threw a linen blazer on, and headed down Florida's A1A ocean highway to West Side's offices.

I'm not sure how it is I came to live in a land of pink palaces and perpetual sunshine. It doesn't suit my personality. But when Lou moved down here from New York, he took me with him. He came for the fishing and the sunshine. He came to get away from New York after Helen died. And I came because he did.

I climbed out of my mint-condition Cadillac that I

bought for a song from the estate of an elderly man who had died. His kids wanted cash. Bargains abound in Florida if you don't mind owning stuff that belonged to dead people. When Lou first saw it, he thought I was nuts. "A banana-yellow Caddy? You like driving fruit?" But I have claustrophobia. I drive luxury land tanks.

Pressing the elevator button for the seventh floor, I rode up in glass to West Side's offices.

"Morning, Cassie," Troy, the receptionist/junior editor, greeted me.

"Mornin'," I mumbled.

"You look a fright."

"Thanks."

"Don't mention it. Coffee?"

"Intravenous."

"You got it." He held out a mug. "Start with this cup, and I'll bring a fresh one in as soon as it's brewed."

I opened the door to Lou's office without knocking.

"This better be worth it. I'm feeling *very* bitchy today," I said, putting the mug down on a mahogany coffee table covered with books West Side had published, and flopping onto a long, buttercream leather couch.

"And how is this different from any other day?"

"If I wanted insults, I would call my mother."

"Guess who called me in the middle of the night?"

"What is it with authors and the middle of the night, Lou?"

"Indulge me."

"John Updike?"

"Bigger."

"I have no clue," I leaned up on one elbow and took a swig of coffee.

He took the unlit cigar he had in his mouth and set it in his Waterford ashtray.

"Roland Riggs."

"Holy shit!" I said, as hot coffee sprayed out of my mouth.

2

Lou smiled at me. "I thought that would grab ya!"

The shock hit me as I mopped at coffee dribbling down my chin. I managed to sputter, "What'd he want?"

"You *do* know my famous Roland Riggs story, right?"

"Do I know it? I've been subjected to your Roland Riggs story at every cocktail party you and I have ever attended together. Worse, I've been subjected to it second-hand from people who have heard the story and feel the need to tell me. They usually embellish it."

Troy came in with my second cup of coffee.

"Thanks." I sucked down a long swig, burning my tongue.

After Troy shut the door, Lou feigned hurt feelings, "All right. So you've heard the story. Well . . . Roland Riggs calls me up in the middle of the night and says—get this—'Lou, I guess I was wrong about the computer.'"

* * *

Lou's Roland Riggs story was this: In 1968, Lou was on a fishing trip in Key West. He caught not a single tuna after two days of deep-sea fishing with Key West's best captain, and he decided to forget the mahi-mahi and settle in for a nice, long beer binge. Lou was sitting at an outdoor patio bar downing a bottle of imported German beer when a disheveled guy about Lou's age sat down next to him and said, "The Germans are the only ones who can brew beer that doesn't taste like piss."

Lou was already a publishing hotshot back then. He knew it was Riggs, even though the author had grown a full beard since his back jacket photo was taken. Roland Riggs, even then, was considered the voice of a generation. He was notoriously moody with his publisher, but he wrote *Simple Simon* and the world had been waiting to see what he would do next. The book sold out of every printing and still does a brisk business. It's required reading in nearly every high school English course. Roland Riggs hit the lottery with his tale of lonesome angst and war and the end of the 1950s and all its innocence and conformity and fumbled sex in the back of Dad's borrowed car.

The two of them started talking. They began with Riggs's dissertation on German brew-making skills. They moved on to discuss women (discovering they both preferred moody brunettes), music (they both despised anything pseudo-folkish with a tambourine in it), books (no one but Riggs, Faulkner, and Hemingway was worth a damn), society's ills (marijuana should be legalized), the price of fame (people like Riggs needed to grow ridiculous beards to avoid strangers accosting them) and the cost of the Vietnam war (the soul of the United States). They started talking on a Friday night at ten o'clock and didn't stop until lunch on Sunday. The last words of their conversation were about the future of technology.

Lou said, "Mark my word, Riggs, one day everyone is going to have a computer—even you. It's gonna change the way we do everything. Even publish books."

Riggs had stared out at the ocean, his blue eyes mirroring its color. "I'll never give up my typewriter, Lou. You've had too much German beer."

With that, the brilliant Roland Riggs stood up, bowed to Lou, and walked down to the turquoise, smooth ocean. He took off his shirt and dove into the water. After splashing about for ten minutes or so, he came out, shook himself like a shaggy dog, and walked, bare-chested, down the beach and out of sight.

"After thirty-some-odd years, Roland Riggs remembered the last words of your conversation?"

"It was a life-changing weekend, Cassie. I remember it."

"You remember it because it was Roland Riggs. But if he was some faceless beachcomber, you wouldn't remember a word of it."

"You underestimate me." Lou stood and crossed the room, barefoot, to his bookshelf. When Lou moved to Florida, he gave up suits. And shoes. He wore flip-flops to the office and then took them off once inside West Side's plush, royal-purple-carpeted suite. He encouraged bare-footedness in all his employees: "It's good for the sole… get it?"

He pulled down his worn copy of *Simple Simon*.

"This book changed people's lives."

"Lou, where's your cynicism? One call from this guy and you're misty-eyed. A generation of child-men went through a war, and he gave them a voice. But life-changing? This from the man who gave a contract to Eliza James because she claimed to have sucked Lyndon Johnson's dick."

"You're too young to appreciate what this book meant. I remember people weeping over this damn book. Let Stephen King do that."

"Danielle Steel makes people weep."

"Danielle Steel, even with a brain transplant, could never win the Pulitzer."

"Fine. I concede the book was important. Brilliant. But when I read news stories about Riggs I feel sorry for him. He hated the attention."

Young men, legless and haunted after Vietnam, camped out in front of the Manhattan apartment where Riggs lived. Their pictures, in their wheelchairs lined up outside his Upper Eastside address, made *Life* magazine. They wrote him bags of mail. But Riggs seemed spooked by the attention his book garnered. He had his glamorous young wife, Maxine, and she was all he needed. Or wanted. They pulled up stakes and moved to rural Maine. He was working on his next book. That would be how he communicated with his public. Through his words. And he would have kept communicating if Maxine hadn't been killed.

Maxine was the literary world's equivalent of Jackie Kennedy. An eighteen-year-old free spirit when they met, she married the handsome, long-haired Riggs when she was nineteen and he was thirty. With long black hair and eyes described as emerald-colored, she dressed with grace and style, and beguiled the rare interviewer with witty comments and an infectious laugh. But after the veterans started seeking them out, Maxine and Riggs retreated to their home and sightings of them became gossip column fodder.

The papers reported it as a tragic accident. She had been standing outside the back door of their white clapboard house, when a trespassing deer hunter shot her. One minute she had smiled at Roland, saying she would go pick them some tomatoes for their dinner salad. The next she was a bloody heap a few feet from her carefully tended garden. Deer bullets leave gaping holes. The hunter never came forward. No one was ever charged.

Roland Riggs's hair had turned completely white by her funeral. He aged ten years in four days. Within a week, he closed up his house in Maine and took off for parts unknown. He never published his next book. He never spoke to the press. He was never heard from again by anyone but his editor. Then his editor died of old age, and no one heard from him except his publisher's royalty department.

"He said I'd understand," Lou looked down at the dust

cover to *Simple Simon.* "He read the article in *Publisher's Weekly* about West Side. How I came here after Helen died. Cassie, he wants *me*...*us*...to publish his next book."

I thought, briefly, of falling off the couch for effect, but I stayed in my seat and struggled to sound intelligent. "Why you? Because you're a widower?"

I stared at Lou. What little hair he had left was silver, and he wore gold wire-rimmed glasses. Short, with a slender build, he would be thought of as elegant. Until someone heard him open his mouth. Then "New Yawkese" came flying out. "Fuck if I know, really, kid. He talked about that night in Key West. How we had a connection. He talked about finding his wife by their garden. He said, 'I've been living with her ghost for over twenty years. She never leaves me. And it never gets better.'" Lou looked up at me. "That's how I feel about Helen."

"I know," I whispered.

"So he doesn't want some faceless schlub somewhere handling his book. He wants me. West Side. Us. If he reads *PW,* he knows how publishers just gobble each other up. Soon, there's just going to be one giant God damn publishing house, and every book will be owned by the same fucking conglomerate. In this day and age, no one will give him the kind of attention he deserves."

"Bullshit. This is Riggs. This is the encore to *Simple Simon.* Publishers would sign their souls over to Satan for a chance to publish it. Just show 'em the dotted line."

"That would imply that they have souls."

"They'd give him a two-million-dollar advance. They

would. What kind of advance can you give him? Our standard fifteen thousand?"

"Well…actually, he doesn't want an advance. He just wants a lot of control."

"Control?"

"Specifically?" He raised his eyebrows, something he does when he's about to tell me news I may not like. Raised eyebrows, edit this book in two weeks.

"He wants you to edit his book."

My heart stopped beating, I think, and in the silence I heard the clock on Lou's shelf ticking.

"Me?" I started breathing again. "He's heard of me?"

"You were in the article in *PW*."

"I'm flattered, but it's not as if I'd let you give his book to anyone else."

"Glad you feel that way." Pause. Raised eyebrows. "Because he wants you to go stay with him while you do it."

"What?" I put my mug of coffee down.

"Yeah. He wants you to move in for a month. Really hash it out."

"Hash it out?"

Lou shrugged.

"Hash it out with Roland Riggs? You don't hash things out with a Pulitzer-prize-winning genius."

"A minute ago you were griping that *Simple Simon* meant nothing. That it didn't change people. That they'd weep over my laundry list."

"A minute ago, I wasn't Roland Riggs's new editor. A minute ago, I wasn't leaving my beachfront condo for who knows where to go *live* with this recluse, who, for all I know, is certifiable after all these years. Christ, he called you up in the middle of the night mid-stream in a thirty-year-old conversation."

"Cass, even if he is certifiable, you'd chew him up and spit him out with your first cup of coffee. Besides, you've handled Michael Pearton. He's not exactly small potatoes. He's hit the *New York Times* bestseller list. Albeit infrequently. God, he takes a long time to write a book. Anyway, Pearton's kind of weird. How bad could Riggs be?"

"Michael's different."

"Yeah. You give him phone sex."

"You know, I told you that over a pitcher of margaritas, and you insist on throwing it in my face every chance you can slip it into a conversation."

"I think it's funny."

"Funny? The guy calls me at three in the morning. He won't let me be. He hounds me with e-mail."

"And he's made you and me rich."

"Technically, you're a lot richer than I am."

"But for thirty-three years old, you ain't doing so bad. And that's nothing compared to what Roland Riggs can do for you."

"And you."

"Sure. But it's not about the money. It's about *Simple Simon*. It's about closure for an entire generation of people who read his book and can't forget it."

"Maybe an encore isn't so smart."

"Maybe it is."

"Lou, what did *Simple Simon* mean to you? Maybe that's what some of this is about."

He looked away.

"Okay, Lou. You don't want to look at that, fine. But it's not like I can just leave all my other authors and books for a month."

"We have e-mail. Take your laptop. You're not in the office all that much anyway. The guy has a phone."

"I don't know. It just sounds . . . weird."

"It's not like you'll be living in a shack somewhere."

"Well, where *will* I be going?"

"He has a big house over on Sanibel Island."

"Sanibel? I'll die there."

Sanibel is a tiny spit of an island off the West Coast of Florida in the Gulf of Mexico. The Old Guard are strict about development. No high-level condos. No good rye bread. No NY-style cheesecake. No nightlife. Lord knows what kind of coffee I could get there.

"He has a housekeeper who doubles as his personal chef. He's right on the beach. You'll have your own guest suite. He has a pool."

"You make it sound like I'm going to the Hilton."

"Look, Cassie, we haven't had a mega-hit in a while. I field calls every month from publishers who want to gobble us up. I'm getting old. I'm not sure I can keep up this independent thing forever. I need this book. *We* need this book."

"You couldn't sell West Side. You wouldn't sell. This is your baby."

"Baby or not, things are tight. We've had a couple of bombs. That damn actress's book—why'd I buy it? So we're in trouble, and I need you to pretend you're going to Vegas. You're going to Vegas, and you're taking all our chips and you're putting them all down on black. In the big roulette wheel of publishing, this is our chance to create a legacy. To leave our mark."

"I need another cup of coffee. I need to talk to Grace about handling my shit while I'm gone. I have to make a dozen phone calls. I've had no sleep. I haven't eaten. And I'm really cranky."

Lou cocked a smile at me. "Just another day at the office." When he smiled, which was much rarer than when Helen was alive, he was still that good-looking kid from Doubleday who made a name for himself by working longer and harder and smarter than anyone else. His blue eyes shone.

I winked at him and went to my office. I slipped off my shoes. Lou's habits had become remarkably enmeshed with my own. I started my personal coffeemaker—I don't work and play well with others, and I don't share my pots of coffee. As I heard the sounds of brewing ecstasy, I leaned back in my chair and put my perfectly pedicured feet up on my desk—"Cherry Poppin' Red" nail polish on my toes. What do you pack to go see a Pulitzer-prize-winner? Do you let him see you before your first morning cup of coffee?

I stared out the window at the Atlantic Ocean that a few hours ago I had described to Michael. Now, everything was different. I was taking all our chips and betting on black.

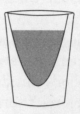

3

Michael took it rather badly.

"What do you *mean* you are jetting off somewhere for a month. A bloody month! We're in the middle of my novel, Cassie."

"Michael, as I've already explained, I have e-mail. Use it. I am taking my laptop. You can leave messages for me at the office, and I can call you whenever you need me. You have written seven books. *Aces High* sold out of three printings and is still doing well. You can handle this little, teensy-weensy inconvenience."

"No, I can't."

"Michael, we're already an ocean apart."

"Precisely why I am so upset with you, Cassie Hayes."

"I don't quite see where we're going with this. You live

in London. I live in Florida. We've worked together for five years. What's another three hundred miles' difference?"

"Cassie, some author calls Lou in the middle of the night, and you're running off to live in this man's house for a month, when you've never even agreed to come to London."

"Well, you've never come to Florida."

"I have. You were in L.A., remember?"

"A poorly timed trip, Michael."

"Why won't you even tell me who this chap is?"

"I can't. I really can't. He's very famous but very protective about his privacy. Lou would kill me. I just can't."

As we talked, I threw the entire contents of my closet on my bed and started picking through my clothes and placing them in pack/don't pack but keep/Goodwill piles.

"You could bloody fall in love with this man. A month! A month in the tropics."

"Michael…" I spoke soothingly, as one might speak to a man about to jump from London Bridge. "I live in the tropics all the time. The warm, balmy breezes are not going to make me take leave of my senses."

"A month in his *home,* Cassie."

"Trust me on this one. I am not going to fall in love with him. Michael, this is ludicrous. And if I did fall in love with him, which I won't because he's too old for me anyway— it's not like I'd ever stop working or stop being your editor. I'm not exactly the stay-at-home wifey type. Believe me. So this entire conversation is predicated on a fear that will never happen."

"I could care less if you stopped being my editor. I want you to come to London."

"Why? So you can feel like you're just as important to me as this author? You know you are."

"No."

A long silence followed.

"Michael? Are you still there? Or have you been drinking, because you are acting totally off the wall."

"For such a brilliant girl, Cassie, you can be impossibly thick as a plank."

More silence.

"Are you so bloody stubborn that you are going to make me say it?"

"Say what?"

"That I am hopelessly besotted with you."

My breath left me. I sat down on the Goodwill pile, and a belt dug into my ass. I moved over to the keep-but-don't-pack pile. More silence.

"So I want you to promise me you won't go doing anything stupid like falling in love with this decrepit old author you're racing off to see—if he really is as old as you say he is."

"I promise," I whispered.

"And I want you to come to London when you return. Even if it's just for a few days. A weekend."

"Michael, what time is it there?"

"Seven o'clock."

"You have been drinking. You're slurring your speech."

"Not a drop."

"I don't understand."

"Yes, you do."

"But...but we have a perfectly good working relationship. I'll grant you that we have phone sex that, well, quite
frankly, is more of a relationship than I have with anyone
else. But why would we ruin this all by meeting?"

"Because you can't love someone over the phone and
over your bloody e-mail. I want to meet you. This has been
the longest pre-coital relationship in history."

"I don't know about that. I think one of the Brontë sisters corresponded with her future husband for seventeen
years or something drawn out and Victorian like that."

"You're not a Brontë."

"No, I suppose not."

"Promise me you'll think about it."

"I promise. But you think about it, too. We have the perfect relationship."

"Long distance?"

"Yes. You know how grumpy I am. How I don't rise before noon. How I need my coffee and have horrible eating habits. I have a two-bedroom condo and live alone, and
I need a weekly housekeeper just to keep the place decent. I laugh too loudly. I drink too much. I play my music
at decibels designed to rupture the human eardrum. I
really am horrible at relationships. 'We,' whatever 'we' are,
are perfect."

"I'd rather have imperfection, Cassie. Think about it."

"I will."

"Call me."

"I will."

"Write me."

"I will."

"And no falling in love."

"Okay."

"Talk to you soon."

"Sure."

"I do adore you."

"Michael..."

"Ciao."

I held the phone, listening to dead transatlantic air until the operator informed me it was time to make a call. What had just happened? A perfectly good editor-author relationship had gone up in flames. How could he love me? We'd never met, as he so stubbornly kept pointing out.

In the past, I'd stared at his cover photos feeling mildly like a jellyfish and woozy inside. He was sexy. But he was there, and I was here. It was perfect. No morning chit-chat. No fighting over toilet seat lid etiquette. No one badgering me about my weird hours, my caffeine addiction, my overindulgence in tequila sunrises. No one yelling at me when my gut screamed out over my combined poor habits and I was writhing on the bathroom floor—no "I wish you'd see someone about that." Michael was my ideal non-lover. And if he thought about it long enough, he'd realize it, too. I'd just let it all sink in to him. Maybe he was having a post-writer's block orgasm from our most recent phone call.

I turned my attention to the serious pile of Goodwill

clothes amassing on my bed. I hated to shop but realized I didn't have a month's worth of clothes to take. Time to hit the mall, then visit my father.

In a place where pink palaces reign, the malls are enough to make a practical woman don a burlap sack. Overpriced is a mantra, and over-the-top is a Boca staple. I pulled up to Bloomingdale's and forced myself to go through the doors. I am seriously mall-phobic. I think it's those faintly *Night of the Living Dead*-like makeup counter women. I'm fond of my slightly flawed face the way it is—crooked smile, full lips, and freckled nose included. I even like the tiny scar by my right eyebrow where Billy Monroe stabbed me with a pencil during a second-grade fight. Billy ended up with a black eye. I called it even.

My shopping technique is simple. I head to Ann Taylor and find a shirt I like. Then I buy it in seven colors. Next I find pants I like. I buy three of the exact same pair in the same size, eight. I do the same with shorts. I toss a scarf and a new purse on the pile. Buy two pairs of size-nine shoes that look comfortable. I don't try anything on. I have them ring it all up. I am out the door in less than fifteen minutes. The Ann Taylor girls see me coming from three stores away and sound some sort of "Bitch alarm." They steer clear of me ever since I told the manager, "Look, I am about to spend seven or eight hundred dollars. I don't want any help. I don't want anyone to talk to me. If you stay out of my way, then I will return several times a year to spend roughly the same amount of money. Deal?" She had nodded, and I've been shopping there for four years.

After damaging my credit card, I left the mall and drove to Stratford Oaks Assisted Living Facility.

"Mornin', Charlie." I smiled at the security guard in the fern-filled lobby.

"Mornin', Ms. Hayes."

I had hoped to be able to really talk to my father, but today wasn't going to be one of those days.

"Sophie!" He smiled broadly at me and called me by my mother's name. I hate that I look like her.

"Jack." I smiled warmly, approaching him, this half-stranger who no longer knew me by my real name most of the time. He looked thinner by the day. They told me he resisted all foods but pie. Why pie? They used to go to some place down in Greenwich Village and order pieces of it after the theater.

"Come here, Sophie. I have to tell you the funniest story."

I listened to his tales of authors and editors in New York's 1940s literary circles. My father had worked for Simon & Schuster. I laughed where I was supposed to laugh and feigned shock where I was supposed to feign shock. I had heard all these stories many times before. "Sophie" patted his bony hand and smiled and went along with the whole charade. I waited patiently for a moment when lucidity would peek through like a ray of sunshine streaming down from behind a cumulus cloud. Sometimes I was rewarded, feeling like some people do when they see a magnificent beam filtering down—that perhaps there is a God in heaven after all. Other times, the clouds stubbornly shut out the sun, leaving both Dad and me in dreary grayness.

"Well, Jack, I really must be going."

"So soon, Sophie? So soon? Our time together is always so brief. I wish your divorce was final."

"It will be soon, Jack. Then we can be together always."

The doctors tell me not to go along with his fantasies. "Bring him back to the present," they say. But I refuse to deny him these afternoons of happiness. He always remembers the same years. My mother and he were dating. It was before I came along. Before she abandoned us both. Before all the heartache.

"I love you, Sophie."

"I love you, too, Jack."

The clouds parted.

"For heaven's sake, Cassie, how long have you been standing there?"

"Only a minute or two, Daddy."

"Come give your Dad a big old hug."

I grabbed him tightly, smelling his Royal Copenhagen cologne, rubbing my face against the soft terry-cloth of his blue robe.

"How's my genius daughter?"

"Just fine, Dad. Guess what?" I said, sitting down on the hassock by his slippered feet.

"What?"

"I'm going to work with Roland Riggs."

He leaned back in his chintz chair and smiled.

"As if you hadn't before…but, my God, Cassie, you've hit the big time."

"I know. And I'm going away for a few weeks. To stay

with him while we work on his new novel. He lives on Sanibel Island."

"Bring me back a conch shell."

I laughed. "I will. Can you believe it? Roland Riggs!"

We talked for about a half hour. I held on to every clear word. Then I could see him growing tired.

"I really need to get going, Dad."

I leaned over and hugged him again.

"I love you."

"I love you, too. And I'm very proud of you."

"I know, Dad. I know."

I fought to keep the tears from coming and stood.

"Tell me everything when you return."

"I will."

"Don't forget a thing."

"I won't, Dad." I smoothed the hand-knitted afghan over his legs and held onto his hand one last time.

Then I walked down the linoleum floors of the hallway. Royal Copenhagen was replaced by antiseptic hospitalish clean. "I won't forget a thing, Daddy," I whispered. I wished he wouldn't either.

4

"Laptop?"

"Check."

"Bathing suit?"

"Lou, this really isn't necessary."

"Bathing suit?" he said, his voice a little more insistent.

"Check." Lou was going to send me off with the precision of a military operation. We stood in the parking garage of my building, his black Jaguar next to my yellow monstrosity. Looking like we'd just completed a mob hit, we stared into my trunk.

"Pajamas?"

"I brought a kimono."

"No can do. Pajamas, Cassie. You cannot sleep naked in Roland Riggs's house. What if there's a fire?"

"You've become a freakish version of a Jewish grand-mother."

"Pajamas?"

"Robe."

"Well, I knew this would happen. So hold on…" He went to his car and fumbled in the front seat. "Here." He smiled, shoving a Victoria's Secret pink-and-white shopping bag at me. Inside was a very tasteful and elegant set of lounging pajamas.

"What? No oversize *South Park* sleepshirt?"

Ignoring me, he continued. "Cell phone?"

"Check."

"Daytimer?"

"Check."

"Coffeemaker?"

"Check." We had decided I should have my own coffeemaker in my room so I wouldn't have to greet Roland Riggs in the mornings pre-caffeine.

"Coffee beans."

"Check."

"Grinder."

"Check."

"Double latte with two sugars for the road?"

"No…I figured I'd stop on the way."

"If you stop, you'll be late. Can you this once be punctual? Hold on." Again he bent into the Jag and emerged with a tall double latte from my favorite coffee bar.

"You happen to have a tall, dark, and handsome guy in there who also cooks?" I took the latte and set it on the roof of my Caddy.

"No. But I thought of everything else. That's why we're a good team."

He smiled at me, and we had another one of our awkward moments. I knew he thought of me as a daughter. He and Helen never had children. But she had always been the one with the easy, affectionate gestures. A tall, graceful blonde, with the aura of Grace Kelly, she was the one who bought my Christmas gifts—always something truly personal and perfect. A first-edition copy of *The Sun Also Rises*. An antique cameo pin for my blazer lapel. A tortoiseshell-and-silver brush-and-comb set engraved with my monogram. Helen gave sentimental gifts chosen to show how much she and Lou loved me. Without Helen, Lou faced the daunting prospect of conveying his emotions without her. Since her death, he hugged me clumsily. Mumbled when it felt right. Nursed me through self-pitying moments with visits to our favorite dive bar. But Helen had humanized Lou; they were a perfect pair, and without her he was totally adrift.

"The best team in publishing." I hugged him. We were about the same height. He patted my back.

"Call me."

"I will. You're going to miss me." I pulled away.

"Oh sure. You after two pots of coffee barking at me over the schedules and covers. Hell, I might actually get some work done with you gone." He cleared his throat. "You better get going."

I threw my pajamas in the trunk, donned my Ray-Bans, and took my latte.

"Admit it."

"Yeah, yeah. I'll miss you. Now get going."

I eased my car out of its tight parking space, waved and was on my way, trying not to think of Michael Pearton. But the mind, even my caffeine-hyped mind, doesn't work that way. I drove across the Florida Everglades, heading toward Sanibel Island, and tried—hard—not to think of his voice. But the harder I tried, the more vividly his face and disembodied voice drifted toward me, like a phantom passenger on my soft leather front seat.

I forced myself to think of Lou and *Simple Simon,* which he made me re-read three times. Lou had been impossible since Roland Riggs's call. Every day he had new instructions. "Hook up your e-mail if you can. Right away. Call me the second you finish reading the manuscript. Tell me what he looks like. See if you can find out if he'll do publicity for the book. Is he willing to do interviews?" I hadn't seen him so hyped up by the possibility of a book since he courted movie legend Joan Fontaine to write her memoirs. (She declined.)

"Lou, shut up," I had said. "You're making me nervous. He's just a guy. He pisses standing up like all the rest of you."

"Sometimes I piss sitting down."

"You know, Lou, that's a little more information than I need to know."

"Christ, I get to hear about every time you have your period. We brace for your PMS like it's a hurricane crossing the Caribbean and heading dead-on towards Boca. You can hear about how I sit."

I smiled to myself as I drove. Think of Lou and Roland Riggs—was I talking to myself already?—not Pearton. I flipped on my stereo, popped in my Elvis Costello CD and steered toward Alligator Alley while listening to "Indoor Fireworks."

Alligator Alley is a lonesome, flat expanse of highway stretching from one coast of Florida to the other. As far as the eye can see in any direction is Everglades. Reeds and swamp, the occasional scruffy tree. I presume alligators. And dead bodies. Mafia hits take place in the 'glades. At least that's what Joe "Boom-Boom" Grasso told me. We published his book about life in the Gambino crime family.

Empty mile after mile of swamp ate at my nerves. I gave up and allowed Michael to invade my thoughts. The mark of a good editor is an anal-retentive mind that never forgets a detail. With my typical obsessiveness, I replayed every conversation I'd had with Michael over the last five years.

So much of what passed between us was banter at first. Indoor fireworks. But somehow, over the years, we had progressed to intimate all-nighters about God (he tried to persuade me to give up my agnosticism), writing, dreams, Freud (we both concurred—sometimes a cigar is just a cigar), and even my father and mother. I forced his face from my mind by singing along with Elvis. Every time I tried too hard to make Michael vanish, he returned to my thoughts, his enigmatic smile staring up from his jacket photo. I felt my stomach tighten slightly.

Two hours after my departure from Boca, my banana-mobile and I emerged from the 'glades and proceeded toward the island. If you're into the beach and the sun and palm trees and sand—which I am not—then Sanibel is indeed a paradise. I hadn't yet spoken to Roland Riggs, but he had given Lou explicit directions to his house. For a New Yorker, any directions that start, "Make a right onto Periwinkle Way" bodes ill.

Driving along Periwinkle, one lane in either direction, I cursed the blue-haired in front of me, steering her Caprice with all the agility and speed of an Indy racer on thorazine. At this pace, I took in Sanibel Island. Dairy Queen. A pizza place. A real estate agency. A shell shop. Not a coffeehouse in sight. No bar I'd consider calling my home away from home. I'd never survive a month.

I followed the directions, winding my way to the water, finally arriving at an immense wrought-iron gate. I couldn't even make out a house. Grasses and dune-like mounds of sand blocked my view. Climbing out of my car, I approached an intercom mounted on the gate. I pressed a button and waited. I pressed again.

"Hello?" A female voice answered.

"Hello. This is Cassie Hayes. Is this the home of Roland Riggs?"

"*Sí*. Hold on."

The gate buzzed and swung open. I got back in my car and drove through. The driveway—if you could call it that—was gravel and sand and meandered its way to an immense house that stood on top of a dune but was perched on stilts like a heron.

I parked at another iron-filigree gate that led into a garden. Leaving everything in my car, I pushed on the gate, surprised at how nervous I felt. I was coming face-to-face with one of the literary giants of the century. Barbara Walters would have coldcocked Katie Couric and Diane Sawyer for this moment.

5

Above the surf noise of the Gulf of Mexico rippling toward shore, I heard a bubbling, gurgling sound. Glancing around the garden, I spotted a fish pond filled with koi. Flashes of gold-and-white-speckled fish lazily swam, flicks of their tails catching beams of sun. A cat perched on the stone ledge surrounding the pond. All white, with green eyes, it licked its paws and stared at me.

"Hey cat," I said, offering it a nod. Then I noticed at least ten other cats sprawled throughout the garden. Orchids hung from tree branches—white and hot pink and purple, all in full bloom and thriving. Other flowers and bushes exploded with a blend of scents—citrus and jasmine. Fruit trees and avocado trees grew, limes and oranges and nectarines ripe for the plucking. Azaleas and gardenias grew—not an easy feat in Florida. Cedar benches and a glider nestled near particularly restful spots. Someone clearly loved gardening. It was a monumental task to coax these flowers to grow in the brutal Florida sun... and the sandy soil. Riggs must have trucked in a farm-full of real soil.

I approached the house, for the first time really noticing its size. Made of glass and stone and wood, it offered views of the water on three sides. A frosted glass-and-wood door, surrounded by hanging orchids, stood atop a narrow slate and rock staircase. I climbed the stairs, rang the bell, and waited.

Finally, the door swung open, and there stood America's greatest living author. Roland Riggs was white-haired and tall. I'd forgotten no one had seen a picture of him since 1977. He wore round silver spectacles that accentuated his clear, blue eyes. His skin was tanned but wrinkled and he smiled, revealing pure white teeth and a pair of craggy dimples. He looked like a vision of America's perfect grandfather.

"Cassie Hayes." He extended a liver-spotted, wrinkly hand and firmly shook mine.

"Yes, sir."

"Call me Roland... where's your stuff?" He craned his neck.

"In my car, down by the garden gate."

"We'll get it later. How's lunch sound? Maria has cooked a plate of enchiladas."

"Terrific."

"Splendid." He turned and led me into his house. He had a slight shuffle to his gait, and his shoulders stooped a bit. His white hair stood up on its ends, a bit of an Einstein-do. I couldn't help but notice he was barefoot. He was wearing a pookah shell necklace. Checkered boxer shorts peeked beneath a pair of crisply ironed tan shorts. The Bee Gees were playing on his stereo. As "Staying Alive" pulsed in the background, I watched him sway back and forth a time or two, involuntarily I think, as people do when lost in a song. He had terrible rhythm. As I followed the man whose words had changed the way America talked about war, I smiled to myself. He wasn't like any grandfather I'd ever known.

Stepping inside Roland Riggs's kitchen was like walking into something out of a Creature-Feature show. Plants didn't just grow in the windowsill, where sunlight streamed in through triple panes of glass. They grew everywhere. In fact, I wondered if a kitchen counter even existed beneath all the plants. It was like *The Day of the Trifids.* Only no Trifids, just plants.

"What *are* all these things?"

"Potato bonsai."

"I beg your pardon?"

"Potato bonsai."

"I've never heard of that."

"Most people haven't. It's an art form. When you were a little girl, did you ever try to grow a potato? Stick one in water with the toothpicks and all that?"

I tried to think back to my childhood. My mother would never have touched a food item that needed cooking. Our housekeeper believed the kitchen was her own

48 *Erica Orloff*

territory and threatened death to all who did not respect her domain. My father? He helped me write a 130-page paper on misogyny in literature for my fifth-grade end-of-year English project. Growing potatoes and other simple child pleasures were not in his repertoire. But I was meeting the famous Roland Riggs for the first time. So I did what I do so well with all my authors.

"Of course," I lied.

"Well, Maria takes it one step further. She tends to these little potatoes here until she can make bonsai out of them. And then she tends to those. See, over there?"

Sure enough, little bonsai plants sat on a corner of the counter in beautiful glazed Japanese pots. Of course, most bonsai plants I have ever seen—which admittedly is not many—created little scenes of Japanese men fishing or sitting on a bench. Or perhaps no scene at all, just the bonsai curving gracefully. These bonsai each had a unique scene of tiny troll dolls—nude—sitting on high chairs or hugging each other, with their trademark Don King fright hairdos sticking straight up in an array of colors from green and yellow to a blinding hot pink.

"This is an art form I have never seen before," I commented. Truthfully.

"She's quite amazing. And now…" He smiled and led me to a beautiful oak-plank table in the dining room. "You get to partake of her other art form. Cooking. Maria is from Mexico, and she is unparalleled in her cooking skills. More evidence of her artistry," he said, with a flourish of his hand.

Ten minutes later, I was tasting the enchiladas. My mouth was burning. Maria, his housekeeper, apparently cooked with a bottle of hot sauce in her belt like a Mexican gunslinger. Only she was slinging fire.

"You like them?" Roland asked from across the dining-room table, polished to a sheen. We could have fit sixteen around it.

"Like them?" My eyes watered, and my voice was hoarse with tears. "I need cold liquid. Ice."

I hadn't yet seen Maria. I assumed she was cleaning in some other part of the house. Perhaps she was trying to kill me. And Roland Riggs.

Genially, he rose and walked over to the refrigerator, one of those blend-into-the-cabinetry custom-made types. *Simple Simon* apparently provided quite an income to Riggs.

"Beer? Cold soda? Ice water? Juice?"

The moment of truth. Let on that I was a coffee-slugging, tequila-loving hedonist? Well, there was no way I was going to hide all my bad habits for a month.

"Beer."

He came over to the table with two Coronas and two lime wedges.

"How's Lou?"

"Good. He sends his best. I actually need to call him and set up my laptop and e-mail if that's okay."

"I never thought the computer would be so big. The Internet... do you know they have over a hundred Web sites devoted to me? That puzzles me."

"You're an enigma. You disappeared."

"Yes, but they post fuzzy photos of me...supposedly me. Someone who vaguely looks like me. One hundred sites..." he shook his head from side to side.

"Anytime someone pulls a disappearing act, seems like people can't handle it. For God's sake, how many idiots out there think Elvis is still alive?"

"You mean he's dead?"

I choked on my enchilada but then spotted a twinkle in his eye.

"You know what I do sometimes?" he asked.

I shook my head.

"I invent a name for myself, and I bash myself on the Web sites."

"Really?"

"Sure. I make up a chat room name like 'Simonsucks' and I visit the Web sites and post how I think *Simple Simon* is a load of crap."

"What happens?"

"I get flamed, of course. People send me all kinds of terrible e-mail. No one has ever caught on that it's me."

He looked quite pleased with himself. I took in a breath. "God, these enchiladas are hot. Aren't you having some?"

"Shh. No, I'm not hungry. Maria is a blessing, but this hot food is all she cooks. I can't cook at all, so I...make do. But Maria makes a fuss when I don't eat what she puts in front of me. A mother hen kind of thing. So keep a secret and say I ate a few." With that he went into the kitchen and took a clean plate from the cabinet and started rinsing it under the faucet. "I put it in the drying rack, and she thinks I ate."

Next he took two enchiladas from the casserole dish they had been baked in and dumped them down the garbage disposal, running it swiftly while looking over his shoulder.

"You know that night a long time ago when you met Lou?"

He nodded and walked back to the table.

"Did it really last a weekend? A three-day bender?"

"Near as I can recall. I do remember thinking Lou was very smart and if I ever wrote a sequel to *Simple Simon* I'd want to work with him. Of course, I didn't think it would take me this long."

"Have you been working on it this whole time?"

"God no. I'm not that pathetic."

"Can I see it?"

"The manuscript?"

I nodded and washed down another burning bite of food.

"How fast do you work?"

"Very."

"Well, then I think we should wait. I want you to understand why I wrote the book first. Otherwise you won't understand it."

"Post-modern?"

"Uh...not exactly."

I lifted my fork, about to subject myself to another bite, when two rabbits appeared from behind a living room chair. They hopped toward the table. I put down my fork and squinted. I blinked. I blinked again. One of the rabbits sat up on its haunches and licked its paws. For a moment, I thought I was hallucinating. Roland turned around to see what I was looking at.

"Oh...those two fellows are Pedro and José. They're Norwegian dwarf bunnies. Siamese. See how they kind of resemble a Siamese cat around their noses?"

I nodded. "And they just hop around the house? Like that? Loose all the time."

"Don't worry. They're not vicious or anything."

I looked at his face, trying to discern how serious he was. Apparently very. His eyes registered concern about my fear of loose rabbits, so I tried to put him at ease.

"I wasn't worried that they're vicious. I...I just never knew anyone who had them just...hopping around like that."

"Later you might see Cecelia. She's a white one. More shy. We think she might be pregnant. They're house-broken, you know."

"Really?"

"Yes. Most of the time. I occasionally find rabbit poop on the bathroom carpet. I keep telling Maria it's because the carpet is green and they think it's grass."

I stood and slowly approached Pedro, who wisely saw I was not an animal lover and hopped away.

"So you like rabbits?"

"I never thought about it, actually."

With that, Maria burst through the door carrying an

armload of fresh cucumbers from an as-yet-unseen vegetable garden.

"Maria, this is our houseguest, Cassie Hayes."

"Hello," she smiled, her black eyes open wide.

"Hi." I was struck by how beautiful she was. She was probably my age. Her dark eyes were framed by jet-black lashes, and her raven hair trailed halfway down her back in a braid. She didn't wear a trace of makeup, and her skin was a deep yellow-brown. Wide cheekbones and a classic nose made her look like an Incan sculpture. At the same time, her hands were rough and chapped as they clutched her vegetables, and she wore ripped jeans and a T-shirt. She was chubby by the standards of *Vogue*. But then again any woman who has actually gone through puberty and grown breasts and hips is fat according to *Vogue*.

"Maria lives in the guesthouse on the other side of the pool."

"Did you eat lunch yet, Mr. Riggs?"

"*Sí*, Maria."

"You, too?" She looked at me.

"Yes."

"You like it?"

More lies. "Delicious." Anxious to change the subject, I asked about Cecilia. "So how many babies do rabbits have at once?"

Maria answered as she started washing and chopping vegetables, "I'm not sure. This is my first bunny birth."

As she chopped vegetables, she set aside a little pile of cut-up pieces. She saw me look at them.

"For my birds."

"Birds?"

"Yes. Sweet birds. Sing beautifully."

I looked at Roland. He silently shook his head. In a moment I knew why. The loudest squawk I ever heard emanated from a sunroom off of the kitchen. It was a cross between a shriek and a banshee howl.

"One minute, Pepito!" Maria glowed. "My babies. Them and Mr. Riggs. Now shoo, I must start cooking dinner. If you liked my lunch, wait until supper. Very hot!"

"Great," I smiled, completely lacking enthusiasm. A month of this and my ulcer would be the size of a crater.

"Let's get you settled in." Roland stood. We went through the gardens to my car and took out my suitcase and bags. Between the two of us, we carried everything in one trip.

Walking back to the house, I forced myself not to stare at him. I was staying with an icon, and part of me remembered when I was a little girl. There were three Christmases I remembered when my mother hadn't yet left, and my father hadn't yet broken down and everything was perfect. The tree was decorated like something out of a Fifth Avenue store window; a toy train chugging beneath it. Our apartment smelled of cider and mulling spices. It was a damn Currier and Ives card. And I remember pinching myself to see if it was real. And when I knew for sure it was real, I tried to remember every detail. I stared and absorbed and thought to myself, even then, that perfect doesn't come along too often. I would remember everything about those Christmases forever. Well, for an editor, Roland Riggs was better than Christmas. He was history, and I was in his house, and when I was old and gray, I wanted to be able to remember everything about my stay. Every painting on the wall. Every word he said. Of course, I needed to remember it all for my nightly reports to Lou. He'd never forgive me if original galleys from *Simple Simon* sat on the bookshelf, and I didn't tell him. Of course, neither one of us expected I'd be staying with Dr. Doolittle.

My room was better than the Four Seasons. It had its own private balcony overlooking the Gulf of Mexico and was decorated in French country, painted in a shade of blue to rival the sea's. I felt almost serene when I stepped inside, though my eyes instinctively darted around, looking for a discreet place to plug in my coffeemaker.

"Over here is a desk...and you can plug in your laptop here."

"Won't I tie up your phone line?"

Roland Riggs leaned his head back and laughed loudly like a drunk in a bar whose bartender has just one-upped him in the joke department. I arched one eyebrow.

"Except for Lou, I haven't called anyone in fifteen years. Maybe my old editor a couple of times. Then he died. But you get the picture."

"Okay fine. So the computer won't bother you."

"No. I surf the Net myself some mornings. Do you get on your computer much before six a.m.?"

"No offense, but I don't breathe much before six."

He roared with laughter again. I realized the unseen parrot was merely mimicking its landlord. "Splendid. Well then, I will let you get unpacked. Take a nap if you want. Stroll the beach. I'll expect you for dinner at six-thirty. Oh...hold on." He withdrew a small roll of Tums from his pocket. "If you thought lunch was hot, you may want to keep a pack of these in your pocket at all times. I have a six-month supply of these little rolls in the linen closet at the end of the hall, behind the big stack of blue guest towels that I never use because I've never had any guests. Until you."

I couldn't help myself. "Wouldn't it be easier to just tell your housekeeper you don't like the food so hot?"

His eyes snapped wide open as if he'd just experienced a moment of sudden enlightenment. He appeared to think for a moment. Then he just shook his head.

"Well, then, I'll see you for dinner." He turned and shut the door behind himself.

I opened the French doors leading to my balcony, and then turned around and raced to the phone. I found my Daytimer, pulled out my calling card and dialed. Lou answered on the first ring.

"Well?"

"Lou, how much money do you think *Simple Simon* brings in?"

"I don't know. A lot. It's required reading in every high school in America. Why?"

"You wouldn't believe this house, Lou. I was sort of ex-

pecting some rundown place inhabited by a hermit. But

sunny and beautiful and *huge!* Right now, I am looking out on my own private balcony. The Gulf of Mexico is rolling in. And he has gardens. Beautiful gardens with orchids and ponds and waterfalls and jasmine. It reminds me of Turkey. The scent of jasmine in the air. And everything is custom-built. The staircase is made of teak. The closet—" I walked over and smelled "—I was right, is cedar. The kitchen—not that I cook—but if I did, I would love it. All restaurant-quality stuff. The stove had eight burners."

"What is he expecting? An army? The guy doesn't see anyone. What's he need eight burners for?"

"What does anybody need excess for? Why do you have seven fishing rods and three sets of custom golf clubs? To have it."

"Well?"

"Well what?"

"How does he seem after all these years?"

"Nice. Kind of odd. The other half of the story is he's got more pets and plants than a zoo and botanical garden put together."

"Pets?"

"Loose rabbits hopping through the house."

"Just so long as you don't tell me he has a Push-Me-Pull-You or whatever that thing is called."

"He has cats. And a parrot. And potato bonsai."

"Potato what?"

"Don't ask."

"Have you seen the book?"

"No."

"Have you talked about it?" I heard the anxiety in his voice.

"Only to have him say he'd like us to spend a few days getting to know each other first."

"Jesus Christ!"

"What?"

"No offense, Cassie, but you are hardly the poster child for Miss Congeniality. What if he's expecting someone different?"

"Well, he's *got* me. And except for that prick Jack Holloway, I've gotten along with every author I have ever had."

"What about Gussbaum?"

"Okay. Except for Holloway and Gussbaum—"

"And Daisy Jones…"

"Look, trust me, he's nice enough. I can get along with Roland Riggs."

"Let's hope so."

"You want to hear something else weird?"

"Of course."

"His housekeeper is from Mexico. She cooks all this food. I mean for lunch she cooked enough enchiladas to feed Mazatlan. And spicy. Burn your mouth out, eyes water, nose-running spicy. I was afraid my nose was going to drip right in my food, for God's sake."

"A little less detail, please."

"But get this. Roland Riggs hates hot food. He carries Tums with him around the house. Isn't that weird? Why not tell her to cook something else?"

"Maybe he doesn't want to hurt her feelings. Remember how your dad used to hate those German dishes what's-her-name cooked?"

"Mrs. Honish?"

"Yeah. He hated all that shit."

"Me, too."

"But she was a good housekeeper except for the food."

"Yeah. Maybe. She's beautiful by the way. The house-keeper. She is take-your-breath-away beautiful. Anyway, let me get going. I have to check my e-mail. Anything earth-shattering on your end?"

"Nothing. It's Saturday. I didn't even go in to the office."

"Okay. Well, I'm just going to take in my view here. Make some coffee."

"Call me tomorrow."

"Or later if I have something to tell you."

"Later, kid."

"Later."

I hung up and unzipped my huge carry-on bag, pulling out my coffeemaker. I plugged it in and set it on my desk and went about preparing a pot. My chest burned. I un-wrapped a Tums and chewed on it. Next I plugged in my laptop and dialed up my e-mail.

PASSWORD: Bitch

LOG-IN CORRECT

I had three messages in my in-box—a light day, but it was Saturday, and most of my authors were aware I was out of town.

The first message was from Kathleen Hawkings. She wrote political commentary and was a frequent guest on

Larry King Live and *Hardball*. She was also very impressed that she was a photogenic blonde who was also bright, and apparently she believed this entitled her to be difficult to everyone in her path.

Cassie:

I am greatly concerned about the size of my author photo on the cover sample you sent me. As you know, I paid Dino Rickman a great deal of money to take those shots, and they came out fabulous. But the photo is way too small. O'Reilly gets a large author photo. So does Tannenbaum. My public will expect this. Please e-mail me immediately and let me know you are taking care of this.

Kathleen

Kathy:

Will have the art department bump it up several sizes. You're gorgeous, of course, and we want the public to see every bit of that face of yours up close and personal.

Cheers,

Cassie

I sent a copy of the e-mail to Manny, our art director, and knew that he would "get" the dripping sarcasm in my e-mail. My Harvard-grad political commentator would not, and that made me simultaneously laugh to myself and grit my teeth.

Where did Lou find these authors?

My next e-mail was from late Friday—my lawyer. It

seemed my mother had pulled a death watch call again. Periodically, she called my attorney to see if my father was still alive because, under the terms of their long-ago divorce, she got a huge lump sum at the time of the divorce and ten percent of his estate when he died. In her mind, the estate was dwindling as I set him up in the nicest assisted living facility I could find. Of course, there was plenty of money left. My hope was that she'd be hit by a bus and die before him, as I saw her pictures every once in a while in *Vanity Fair* on the arm of her latest billionaire husband and she appeared disgustingly healthy. Pictures can lie, I consoled myself. Perhaps she was rotting from the inside out with stomach cancer. One can hope.

The third e-mail was from Michael. I held my breath as I opened it.

Cassie:

I hope I didn't scare you off with my phone call. When you told me you were leaving for a month I just took leave of my senses. Forgive me? But who else can I call in the middle of the night? Who else will talk to me of cold nipples and tequila sunrises and coffee? And tea? Who else would own a tea set worthy of Queen Liz and let it tarnish on her counter? Because I know it's brown as dishwater by now. And I find that all the more endearing. You resist any attempts by anyone to change you. And that's precisely why you are both exasperating and charming. Write me. Call. Tell me you forgive my emotional outburst. Tell me you are coming to London.
Truly,
Michael

I felt a shiver run through me. My coffee was done brewing, and I remembered I hadn't brought a coffee mug. I stood in a panic, crossed the room and poked my head in my bathroom. It was nicer than a hotel's, down to little teeny shampoos and soaps.

"Perfect," I grabbed a large water glass, went back and poured my coffee. I stared at Michael's message. I stared and thought of his voice. Finally, I started clicking at the keyboard.

Michael:

You didn't scare me. In case you haven't noticed, I am not the frightened type. In fact, I am usually the one who does the scaring. If you saw the state I keep my bathroom in, for example, you would be utterly terrified. Toothpaste drippings on the sink. Towels on the floor. Make-up dust on the counters. Hairspray stuck to everything. It's not pretty. If I came to London and did this to your bathroom, you would immediately regret it. The fantasy is so perfect. I have so little in my life that's perfect, Michael. Wouldn't you rather keep it pure? Keep us on the phone laughing and talking and not changing?

I wish I could explain how your face stares at me from the jacket covers. I feel like some little girl who kisses her David Cassidy poster each night. I don't know if you'll get that reference. But you sense what I mean. There is no one else. And this—whatever this is—is ideal. Write. Call. Tell me you know that I am right.

Always,

Cassie

I hit Send. If I went to London and things weren't perfect, there was no send or delete button. Real life was messy. Sloppy bathrooms I could handle. Love I could not.

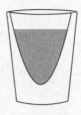

6

I am the only Floridian I know without a tan. Not even a hint of one. It's not that I care that the ozone layer has a hole in it the size of China. I could give a shit about SPFs and suntan lotion. When I do venture out in the sun on that rare occasion, I watch my freckles multiply like rabbits on fertility drugs. But I like my freckles, so it has nothing to do with that. I just hate to slow down.

But here I was in paradise.

I ventured downstairs after sending all my e-mails and felt like I had nothing to do. Probably because I didn't.

"Where's Roland?" I asked Maria as she stood over the stove brewing some concoction with so much onion and garlic and jalapeños in it my eyes flooded with tears.

"Mister Riggs is on the beach. Fishing."

"What time's dinner again?"

"We eat at 6:30 every night."

Trying to make conversation, I offered, "I think it's amazing that you can grow fresh vegetables. There's nothing but sand around here. Between that and your potato bonsai here, you have a regular green thumb. I killed a cactus that I only had to water once a year."

"I learned as a little girl. Only none of the vegetables were for me. We picked them, my family and I. So now I have a garden—Mister Riggs's garden—but I love growing vegetables with my own hands. They taste better."

She held a tomato out in front of her, marveling at its red ripeness. "And I don't have to give them away. They are for my babies. Mister Riggs, and the birds and the bunnies." She turned to smile at me, and then she bent her head over her pan, ignoring me as she worked her sorcery over the stove.

Feeling dismissed by Maria, and with time on my hands and a house that smelled like gastric doom to me, I decided to venture to the sand.

Stepping out on the clean white beach, I spotted Roland in the distance. He cast his line into the Gulf and pulled back. Then cast it again. Over and over, falling into a rhythm. I didn't want to intrude, so I started walking in the opposite direction.

The early evening was breezy. The sun hadn't yet set, but the sand was nicely warm—not too hot—on the soles of my feet. Shells dotted the beach in wavy lines where the tide had brought them in. An osprey swooped down to the water, and dune grasses grew ragged along the shore. I hated every minute of my walk. Time stretched out in front of me like the beach. I couldn't imagine a week here. Let alone longer.

When I was in college, my freshman roommate was a manic-depressive. Cherish, named by her hippie, acid-dropping parents, stayed awake for days on end, the life of the party. She did stupid things like max out her father's credit card—by then he'd started a software company and made millions. She walked up to the biggest football player on campus and called him a Neanderthal after he fumbled the ball on what would have been the winning touchdown in the most important game in the University of Virginia's season. She climbed out on the ledge of our dorm "to look at the stars" at night. She drank too much. She didn't take her Lithium.

In her depressive episodes, Cherish refused to eat. She wouldn't shower. She didn't dress. She curled in a fetal position on her bed and sucked her thumb. Her beautiful chestnut brown hair grew matted. She cut all her classes.

I accepted Cherish for what she was. I would come back to our dorm after classes and stroke her hair and try to get her to eat something. I knew the cycle would reverse itself sooner or later. And it always did.

I never tried to talk her into taking her Lithium, and even though everyone else on our hall thought I was crazy, I opted to live with her again the following fall and every year after that. She wouldn't take her Lithium because it made her lose the highs. And I knew better than anyone how that felt.

She and I called it our sweet insanity. Of course, my

brand was higher-functioning. I never hit the lows and never soared to her highs. My brand was just killer Type-A, pedal to the metal, careening wildly, never-sleep drive and ambition. I graduated second in my class; I double-majored; I interned every year while taking a full load. I worked nights as a bartender. I never stopped. And it was bliss. My Aunt Charlotte accused me of running from something. I thought I was running *to* something. To greatness. To excitement.

After college, I got a job working for Lou. I arrived before 7:00 a.m. and left long after the janitor. He and Helen noticed. Everyone did. Soon, I was lunching opposite the poet Diego Rivera, and working with names I had dreamt about. But, though meeting famous authors and lunching at New York City's hot spots was a kick, it was the pace I craved. If I had gone to medical school, I would have thrived in the E.R. and never bitched about the long hours of residency.

When my father slipped into the past and stopped realizing who I was, I worked longer and harder. Helen used to fuss over me, but she never really expected to get me to ease up. Saint Helen accepted everyone as they were. Lou was more pragmatic, I suppose: "Kid, the only thing that's gonna slow you down is your second heart attack— if you survive your first." Always one to tell it straight.

I breathed in the Gulf air. The beach was nearly empty, and I felt my heart slow down a smidge. I thought of my father.

"This story is good, Cassandra. Very good. I am going to type

*it up and you can illustrate it, and I'll keep it forever. I'll keep
you forever, Angel."*

*He took me up on his lap, and I wrapped my arms 'round his
neck, breathing in his Royal Copenhagen scent. I felt the starchy
crispness of the collar of his Brooks Brothers shirt. He put his hand
to my face and wrapped a stray curl around his pinkie, watching
my jet-black hair circle his finger in a spiral.*

*"You know, I shouldn't say this, but sometimes I'm glad I don't
have to share you with your mother, Cassie. I come home from
work and you run to me, smelling of Johnson's Baby Shampoo,
and I get all the exuberance and all the hugs. All for me. But you
deserve so much better. A mother's touch. We both do."*

*He clasped his arms around me, and I twirled the JJH-initialed
cufflinks in his French cuffs. He stared out the window. Traffic on
Park Avenue was in a five o'clock crawl. But he wasn't really seeing the traffic or me or our apartment. He was seeing her, I knew.
In his mind. I was six years old, and I remember thinking he
looked, for that brief moment, very old.*

"Mind if I join you?"

I was startled by Roland, suddenly at my right side.

"Not at all."

"I asked Lou if I was inconveniencing you by request-
ing that you stay here while we work on the book. He told
me you didn't mind."

"Did he, now?" I cocked an eyebrow.

"He said you weren't married, that you hadn't found a
lucky guy yet, and—"

I laughed. "Mr. Riggs...Roland, I'm sure that's not exactly what he said."

He stopped and kicked at the sand with his toe, smiling. "You're right. Not exactly."

"What did he say exactly?"

"I'm not sure..."

"Come on. It won't be anything I haven't heard before."

Roland paused, clearly assessing whether I really meant I wanted the truth. "Lou said, 'Cassie? She won't even take care of a God damn goldfish. Married? Not likely. She's got nothing holding her here except for her father. She'll come.'"

"Lou's sweet that way."

Roland's eyes twinkled. "So...do you think I'm crazy asking you to come here?"

"No...I don't." I looked at his face, wrinkled, but rosy-cheeked from the sun.

"Cassie, you're a terrible liar."

"Am not. I have an excellent poker face, you know."

"Hmm. Well, I'm not crazy."

"Of course you're not."

"Good. Glad you agree. See you for dinner." And with that he took off toward the house. "By the way," he turned to face me. "Do you like music?"

"Sure. What kind?"

"Oh...I don't know. Classical. Opera. Hip-hop... *Disco.*"

He stared straight at me.

"Disco? Well...I grew up with the Bee Gees, but it's not like I play them all the time now."

"Ahh. But you *did* know them in high school."

"Personally? No. But everyone listened to them."

"Splendid." He turned away. "You better eat those Tums I gave you before dinner. She adds extra spice in the evening. Damn-near kills me every night."

I watched Roland Riggs disappear up the beach, his head bobbing over the waves of grass in the dunes. Yeah. He wasn't crazy. Much.

At dinner that night, my nose ran—so did Roland's—and we kept dabbing at them with our napkins. Maria didn't even have a hint of mucus about her. How can you trust someone who manufactures no phlegm?

Roland clutched his napkin to his nose, then said, "When I was trying to decide what publisher to call, I read all of Michael Pearton's works. I re-read 'Night All a second time. He raved about you in his acknowledgments."

"Michael gets a little sappy."

"Sap's okay."

"Sure. Sap's okay, if you're into sap."

"You *must* be into sap." Roland pounded the table. "Sap is what makes the world go 'round."

He raised his Corona. "To sap."

"What is sap?" Maria asked, hesitantly raising her glass.

"Sap," proclaimed Roland, "is a belief in wishing on a star, in angels and fairy wings. Sap is believing in love at first sight and soul mates. Sap is the only way to go through life. Otherwise the ugliness will wear you down."

"*Sí*. Sap. To sap." She nodded her head, approvingly.

I lifted mine. I couldn't believe I was toasting sap.

After dinner, Roland and I sat in the living room. He could slide all the panes of glass over, making the room open directly out to the Gulf.

"Where's Maria?"

"She has a little cottage on the other side of the pool. She usually changes after dinner, and then comes here and watches a TV show or two. Then she goes back to her cottage and does whatever it is she does."

Roland abruptly stood up and faced the sea. "You know, I held my wife as she took her dying breath."

He turned around to face me and looked as if he might say something more. But then he stared at me expectantly.

"I didn't know." I hoped I was saying what he wanted me to say. "I'm so sorry."

"You've known loss. I can tell. And Lou told me."

"Told you what?"

"Nothing specific. I just asked if you could relate to loss, and he said yes."

I thought about my mother. She had been out of my life so long, I stopped thinking of her absence as a loss and started thinking of it as how it was meant to be. But my father had become a shell of who he once was. I knew loss. "I can."

"But he also said you're not the touchy-feely type."

"I'm not."

"Neither am I. I like a good hug now and then, but I'm alone here, except for Maria, so I don't get the chance. But I do believe in true love. Do you?"

"I'm not sure."

"Hmm. It would be better if you did."

"Better for what?"

"For what we are facing. So that's not good, however in your favor you are very honest."

"I don't believe in bullshit."

"Good. Neither do I. I'm going to go for my nightly walk now. Please feel free to watch television. My *casa* is your *casa,* as they say in Mexico."

He crossed the living room and walked out onto the deck.

"It would help if you believed, Miss Hayes. But I won't force the issue."

With that he disappeared into the darkness.

I felt stupid sitting in a big living room all by myself. I don't watch TV. I went to my room and e-mailed Lou.

Lou:

Help me. Roland Riggs speaks of disco and fairy wings. Where is the man who wrote *Simple Simon,* Lou? I fear his brain has turned to mush here under the stars. Lou, I will go positively insane if I stay the month. I'll do it, but…send bagels. Send coffee. Send me someone who doesn't want to know what I think of Andy Gibb, the Bee Gees, and finding your soul mate. Lou…you always tell me I have the best "gut" in the business. My gut tells me Roland Riggs left part of his mind in a tomato garden in Maine.

I'm bored outta my mind.

And his housekeeper is trying to kill me.
Seriously.
Swear it.
Miss even you,
Cassie

7

I clicked on Send, and my e-mail made its way through cyberspace to Lou's computer where it would remain until the next morning. Lou isn't a night owl. Ever since he took up fishing, he is one of those guys who'll get up at the crack of dawn, rod in hand and fish for two hours before most human beings are even out of bed. Only I know it's because he can't sleep with Helen gone. He dozes in front of the television set, but he waits anxiously for that dawn, for that moment when he can bolt his condo and hit the beach and not be reminded that he has a huge expanse of nighttime and no one to fill it with.

Periodically, one of the women at work gets the bright idea of trying to fix up Lou on a date. The inappropriate-ness of this bemuses me. Besides his expansive list of weird character traits and decidedly un-dreamboat-like qualities—the fact that he eats cold Chinese food out of a box for breakfast and won't wear shoes in the office (and his feet are ugly), the way he burps loud enough to wake the dead if he drinks his beer too quickly—there is the little fact that he is nowhere near ready to date. And probably never will be.

ARE YOU THERE?

Sitting at the keyboard, thinking about Helen and Lou, my thoughts were interrupted by an instant message. About a year ago, Michael got the bright idea that we should each have an instant messaging system on our computers so that we could write in real time on the computer on days when we were both bored but I was too crabby to answer my phone or to really be civilized.

Yes.

Are you in love with him yet?

I clicked back:

Who?

The mystery author.

No, I am not in love with him yet. I am not going to fall in love with him.

I pressed the Enter key, and my message zipped to London. No love between Roland Riggs and me. That I knew as surely as I knew dinner would be repeating on me all night long. I unrolled four Tums and chewed them into a big, chalky, fruity-flavored mess in my mouth.

Good. Then I have a chance. Cassie…you know this seduction is with words. This long, slow dance we have been doing for years now. Circling in a tango of words. A dip here. A turn of the heel there. Pulling you in close to me until we both hear the tango at the same time, heart against heart.

When I was a teenager, what a bloody fool I was like every poor besotted fool since the beginning of time. My seductions were all of a fumbling sort. A grape of the

He paused in his writing.

Scratch that. A GROPE of the breast, a silly kiss on the street before I dropped her home. I got older, and my seductions, to be honest, weren't much better. I tangoed much better, of course. I learned about rhythm and pacing yourself during the dance until the breathless finish, but it was still all about a quick grasp of the hand, a fumble in the dark—pull close only to pull away because risking the dance becoming more than a dance was too dangerous.

I read his words, aware he was sitting on his bed, laptop on a pillow, clicking this off the top of his literary head. These were his thoughts. Unedited. Before I ever took hold of them or shaped them. It was the middle of the night in London. Michael is not a good sleeper.

And then there was Cassie. Our dance is so much more frightening. But I cannot be still. I must make you hear our music. Hear the way our words overlay each other's like a scherzo. A perfect composition. And then you must feel. You must feel, Cassie, that we are the sun rising over your ocean, the sun setting over London, two halves. But not two halves. The same sun. Just different horizons. But still one.

Dance with me tonight.

I took a deep breath.

Michael. I hear. I hear the band playing, but you know I never dance. All right. I dance sometimes at weddings. Occasionally when drunk. I dance on tabletops and on top of barstools. A long time ago, at least, I used to do that. But this kind of dance? Trusting that you won't drop me when you dip me? Now you're asking a lot of me. You remain the setting sun over London. This mystery. We dance, but you hold back. And so do I. The fact that you can't call me—it's making you worry. But I'll be back before you know it, and we can continue whatever "this" is.

I pressed Enter. He responded in a flash.

I do not hold back. Tell me what you're wearing.

I looked down at my T-shirt and jeans. Not terribly exciting. I stood up and stepped out of my jeans and pulled off my shirt, unhooking my bra and letting it fall to the floor.

I'm not wearing anything, Michael. For the moment, I am all yours.

My screen blinked...waiting, waiting for his reply.

It drives me mad when I picture you naked. I want to taste you, Cassie. I want to feel your nipple beneath my tongue. I want to start at the hollow of your neck and make my way down to your legs and nestle my head there between them, home at last. That is what I want. That, from the moment we first started writing and calling each other, is all I have ever wanted.

I wrote back:

I think about how your cock would feel, Michael. But the delicious fantasy, this pre-coital bliss is better than anything real between us. Do you really want to grow old together and hate the sight of each other? Do you really want to look across the table and realize the thrill is gone? Maybe the thrill would be there for a while, but it always fades. That is the march of time. It dulls everything. I would rather dream of your cock inside me, than have it and tire of it someday.

I waited.

Love is not a rush of wetness between your thighs, or this MASSIVE erection of mine (have I told you lately how downright sexy I am?). It is what's between your ears. That brain of yours that I must possess.

"You want to play, Michael, but you don't really want to dance," I whispered softly.

Please. What's between my ears is drunk half the time. And what about you? How many times do you call me slurring and out of it, Michael? Is it after you have dropped off a date? Slept with her and been disappointed? Then you dream of me and call, drunk? Tell me, Michael. Tell me why in five years if you felt this way, you have never come to America? You refuse to talk to me about your drinking. You are as interested in preserving this ideal as I am, you just will not admit it. If you would go ahead and ask me some of the questions you must want to ask...but are too afraid of the answers, THEN we could discuss a tango. For now, we just dance on the edge, afraid of truly letting go.

I sent the message, and I waited. I waited minutes. I opened the window of my room and listened to the Gulf of Mexico, knowing I had trumped him. In all our time together, he avoided discussing his drinking. He also pointedly refused to answer whether he was sleeping with all of London.

And then, POP. His words came zapping onto my screen.

I know I sometimes come across as an alcoholic, but I'm not. You, however, well…that's for another night, another e-mail. I wish I could tell you why I have avoided coming to America to meet you. It's a long story, but I assure you it is not what you think. But now that I fear you may slip away into the arms of another man, I must put aside all my fears and tell my secrets and dance finally. With you. My turn for a question.

Here it comes, I thought.

Have you ever thought, even for a second, that you could love me?

Now it was my turn to stare at the keys and think. I grabbed another Tums. I chewed. I swallowed.

Yes. But of course, that's not saying much. I thought I could love Marlon Brando (in his thinner years). And I went through a Mick Jagger phase. When I see his helium lips now I could just smack myself. These were my youthful obsessions/crushes. What was I thinking? I had terrible teenage crushes. So my track record is really abysmal. All my relationships end badly. I can't even have a good one-night stand, Michael. I even tried marriage once. But that's a story for another time.

He typed back:

Tell me.

No. You got your one question. I gave my one answer. Yes. But whether we can dance, Michael, that's for another night. It's nighttime here. Time for me to go to bed.

He still tried to make me love him across the ocean separating us:

Dream of me. Ravishing you. Crawling next to you and making love to you.

I clicked back:

I think I'll actually dream that giant burritos are assaulting me.

I don't understand????????

Long story.

Good night, Cassie. My sun will be your sun tomorrow.

Good morning, then, Michael.

I'll e-mail you later.

Bye.

Bye.

Michael??

I was just about to log off.

Sometimes I wish I wasn't so afraid of dancing.

I logged off my e-mail system. I didn't want to see what he wrote back. I didn't want to dream of Michael. The breeze coming in my window caressed my face. I turned and stared at the huge sleigh bed, as yet unrumpled. I stood, turned off the light and stretched. I had laid out my new pajamas from Lou. The silk felt sinful against my bare legs. Lying down, I felt my heart race. The end of my day— my night, really—is always the same. Try to relax enough to sleep. Drink enough to sleep. Work until exhausted enough to sleep. To stop. To surrender to the Jungian world of dreams and symbols. For me, my dreams are always about falling and running and large alligators hunting me down in subterranean tunnels. And memories long buried. A giant burrito or Michael Pearton? Who would come calling in my dreams? I felt dinner burning a hole in my gut. It would be a very close race indeed.

8

"Big money! Big money!"

Tuesday night was the same as Monday night, which was the same as tonight. I sat wedged on a couch between Roland Riggs and Maria watching *Wheel of Fortune*. The two of them commented on Vanna White's outfit. I found Roland was partial to evening gowns, whereas Maria favored her short dresses with sequins. Lots of sequins. They also disagreed on the question of Vanna's hair. Roland preferred her hair down, with a slight curl. "It makes her more youthful. Flattering to her face."

"No. No, Mister Riggs. She looks much better with her hair up like last night. Don't you think so, Cassie?"

"Hair up? Hair down? These are the mysteries of the ages. I'm with Maria on this one."

"And," Roland said, "while we're discussing the mys-

teries of the ages, why on earth did they stop with the let-
ter turning."

I turned my head to look at him. "Sorry. Apparently I
was in an amnesiac when this controversy arose."

Maria became animated. "She used to turn the letters.
These big lit-up squares. Blocks. Now she just touches the
square—see she's doing it now. She just touches it, and it
lights up. It's like magic! No turning. But, Mister Riggs says
it makes her job seem less important."

A less-important letter-turner.

My life had become a bad Fellini movie.

That morning I had asked him about the manuscript.

"Soon. I promise."

At night, I sometimes heard him in his office very late.
Sounds of a printer churning out pages sparked hope in
me. At least, I mused, the book exists. I hoped so.

After *Wheel of Fortune,* the room became electric with excitement. Alex Trebek and *Jeopardy!* were next. I had dis-
covered on Monday night that Roland was unbeatable. No
one could spout the answer out faster than he—and he always phrased his answer in the form of a question. What dis-
turbed me most was the arguably greatest literary mind of
this century was content to watch game shows. Yet his mind
was apparently sharp enough to recall the Norse tales of the
Norns and the history of 19th-century bridge-building as
he answered the *Jeopardy* thousand-dollar questions. Why
was he staying on this little island when he could be the toast
of New York? He could be the toast of anywhere. Hell, he
could *meet* Vanna White and Alex Trebek if he wanted to.

Wednesday night, as Alex was poised to tell his television audience the origins of the myth of Aphrodite, the phone rang. Curiously, in the five days of weird hell I had spent in the home of Roland Riggs, the phone had never rung.

Roland stared at Maria, who stared back. They both looked at me.

"Well?" I asked. "Are you going to answer it?"

Roland rose and strode to the counter where the phone rested. Lifting the receiver, his voice was tentative. "Hello? Mmm-hmm." He turned to face me, holding out the phone. "It's for you."

I crossed the room. I'd never know Aphrodite's origins. "Hello?"

"Miss Hayes?"

"Yes?"

"This is Carla Waters at Stratford Oaks."

My heart fell somewhere down into my shoes, and I gripped the counter of the breakfast bar to steady myself.

"Is my father all right?"

"Yes, he's fine. And I'm very sorry to bother you. I couldn't reach you at your office, and I spoke to your employer. He's listed on your emergency number list."

"Lou."

"Yes. And...ummm...I told him we had a situation here, and he gave me this number and said you'd want to know."

Situation. It's the kind of word used by stalwart men in dark suits in movies to explain to the president of the

United States that a nuclear war is at hand: "Mr. President...it appears we have a situation."

"Please just tell me, Carla."

"Your mother is here. Was here, actually."

"My mother? Oh my God, did she upset him?"

"No. I don't think so. I talked to his day nurse, Kathy, and she said he seemed fine after she left, but it seemed like he didn't realize they were...you know, divorced. But I know you have express instructions that he is not to receive any phone calls from her. You said phone... But I suppose we didn't think she'd ever visit. She got past the reception desk and was alone with him for about ten minutes."

"That God damn bitch."

"Well, Miss Hayes, I suppose I shouldn't say this, but those very words passed through my mind."

"She's on a death watch." Out of the corner of my eye, I saw Roland Riggs watching me. He was no longer answering Alex's questions.

"I don't understand."

"It's about money. I keep telling her he's going to live a long time, and it'll be a while before she gets her greedy paws on his money. But to tell you the truth, I don't care if I never get a dime from him. As far as I'm concerned, spend the estate on Stratford Oaks. I could care less. I want him cared for."

Carla Waters, a beautiful African-American administrator with a laugh that could charm the very old near-corpses in some of the rooms, was silent. She was a compassionate woman. She had seen, no doubt, the ugliness that families wreak as they claw and fight over pennies as their parents and grandparents wither away and die.

"Please don't let her in again. And I'll call her. I have to call her and tell her she is not allowed to see him. Ever. And please call me tomorrow if he seems upset by this."

"I will. I'm sorry this happened."

"It's not your fault."

"He's a very sweet man, your father is. And he's lucky to have you."

"If you only knew, Carla. I am so much luckier."

We said our goodbyes, and I hung up. My hands were as cold as if plunged in a bucket of ice water. Then the rage came shooting up from my stomach. Rage or the chili-pepper-covered casserole we'd eaten that night.

"Roland? I'm going to go for a walk. I need some air."

"Fine. We'll be here with Alex."

On the beach, darkness was descending. I struggled with an imaginary dialogue of hatred and viciousness designed to wound my mother.

You heartless beast. You're not a mother. You're a sculpture of silicone and collagen.

But I couldn't wound her. That would imply she cared what I thought. In truth, she cared about when her next facial peel could be scheduled. Where she would vacation. With who? Where was Blaine Trump buying her next pair of shoes?

"Am I intruding?" Roland's voice startled me from behind.

"No. Not really. I guess you heard my messy little family situation."

"Partly. Your mother is a bitch?"

"Something along those lines." I stared ahead in the darkness, grateful he couldn't see my face. "She left my father and me when I was a little girl. She was always more interested in her address—that it be Park Avenue—and her couture than she was ever interested in being a mother. Ostensibly, so that she wouldn't look like the offspring-eating monster that she is, she told all her society pals that I was borderline retarded. Couldn't read. Needed a special tutor at the private school I attended. So when she moved in with husband number three, there was no sense in uprooting me across Central Park. I should stay with my father and that way I could get the special attention I needed."

"Points for cleverness."

"Points for evilness."

Crabs scattered across the sand. I could hear their scuttling in the still night.

"Your father is ill?"

"Not really. He has the 'big A.'"

"Alzheimer's?"

I nodded, not knowing if he could see me in the darkness. Not caring, really. Just wanting my mother to be shark bait.

"What are you going to say to her? You do have to call her."

"I don't know."

"My in-laws hated me. Until *Simple Simon* took off and I made enough money to buy my wife a house, I was that good-for-nothing son-in-law. That writer who couldn't hold a day job. Who wouldn't."

"Did you ever confront them?"

"After the funeral. I told them how she used to lie awake at night and cry because they were so judgmental of me. How she and I were soul mates even beyond death and their jealousy of that is what made them hate me."

"Touché."

"Or so I thought. But all these years it's eaten away at me. Inflicting hurt. I can do it. I can harm others with words. But I choose not to now. I don't want that skill anymore. Maria's taught me that."

"To be kind?"

"You could say that. She's taught me to love that garden. The rabbits. Caring for them has saved me, I suppose. Her gentleness. All I know is what I'm capable of, and what I don't want to be capable of. Brilliance, my dear, is a terrible burden. But you know that, of course."

"I'm not in your league."

He put his hand on my shoulder.

"You know that's not true. I can already tell you've spent your life knowing you were smarter than anyone around you. Which is why you cannot abide by *Wheel of Fortune.* Your skin crawls each time a contestant can't fill in the letters and solve the stupid thing. The 'Wheel,' Cassie, is a metaphor for life."

I smiled. "Love the stupid?"

"Perhaps. But never underestimate them."

"I don't understand you, Riggs."

"That's okay, Hayes. You will."

He turned to walk up the beach toward his magnificent house, an example of what brilliance can buy. Then he paused.

"Tomorrow…the manuscript. You know pain."

With that he sauntered up the beach, scattering the crabs as he went.

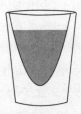

9

The next day around 11:30, I checked my voice mail. They were enough to send me searching for Maria's bottle of Tabasco sauce. I wanted to drink it and put myself out of my misery.

"Hello…Cassie, this is Martin Morris III. I sent you a manuscript entitled *The Secret Life of a Hairy Woman*. I'm not sure if you read it yet. It's about the real-life circus love affair between a clown and a bearded lady. I was wondering what you think…please call me at 555-8773. Area code 562. Thanks. Did I say this was Martin Morris III? I think I told you I was the son of a former circus performer. The Human Hammer. He used to pound nails up his nose. Anyway, call me if you can. Thanks. Martin Morris. Thanks."

The cool modulation of the voice mail seductress told me if I pressed nine I could save my message. If I pressed seven, I would delete it for all eternity. The son of the Human Hammer? That would be a seven.

"Cassie? Jane Marchand here. Look...I absolutely refuse to do another book signing for you-know-which megastore. I got there, and they didn't have a table set up. Some sweating, greasy nerd of a manager with an *actual* pocket protector set up a signing table finally, and then he didn't have enough books. What a schmuck. I am telling you—forget it. No more. Who could put up with this?"

Lucky number seven.

"Cassandra Hayes? Donald Seale from *Conversations* magazine. I think you'll want to return this phone call. It concerns Roland Riggs. I'm staying at the Sundial Resort on Sanibel. We're neighbors you might say. Please call me. It's urgent."

Seven. I felt stalked. How did he know where I was?

"This is Harry, Cassie. I need to speak with you about chapter six. What's with this comment here you wrote about Lucy not being believable? She's horny for the hero. I think it's perfectly legit. And I can't even read your writing on the last page."

Harry...the man writes novels about a swaggering, drinking detective and the women who fuck him. All of the women have breasts the size of the Hindenburg and "gams" with more curves than the Pacific Coast highway. I must have written my comments when I had finally decided he could take his "erect nipples" and "tight little asses" and shove them up his own tight little ass. The se-

ries had started as a very fresh approach to the hard-bit-
ten private eye and had deteriorated to shit.

Press nine. Save it until I could respond with an appropriately specific voice mail of my own.

"Cassie...this is your mother. I went to see your father,
and he looks unwell. I am not sure where you are, but I
would appreciate a status report. You can reach me at the
Palm Springs number. I know you won't call me. You act
as if that man is God, Cassie. Well, I'm your mother, and I
am entitled to know what is happening with him. You
think this is about the estate but—"

Speed up her message. Press seven so hard my index finger turns white.

"Cassie...Michael here. I just wanted to hear your
voice, even if it is your damned machine."

My heartbeat escalated like the disco beat constantly
pulsing throughout the house on Roland's stereo.

"I wish you'd call me. I'm not sure who this famous author fellow is, but he can't possibly need you more than I
do. I can't finish the book without you. I won't, actually.
Call me. I won't write another word until you do. And I'll
hold my breath also."

Silence, but still no beep signaling the end of his message.

"See...I really am holding my breath. I don't think you
want me to pass out. I'm stark naked, and the tabloids
would love it now, wouldn't they? Finding me dead,
naked...they would think I'd been wanking off when in
fact I had been having a tantrum over my beautiful editor. I'm holding my breath....You better call me."

Beep. Message over. I pressed nine. A keeper.

Next message: "Cassie…" Michael again. "I've decided holding my breath is just too damned difficult. I'm going on a hunger strike instead. I'm giving up my bloody bangers and everything. I'll just drink martinis. Just alcohol. No food."

Press nine.

"Cassie…Michael—"

What was it about English accents? His voice sent a shudder through my body. I sat down on my bed and pulled the blanket around me.

"I've decided the hunger strike should not include martini olives. I am going to eat jars of them to sustain myself. And the martinis. Please call."

Press nine. I was smiling and shivering at the same time. But it was time to call Lou. I explained I hadn't even seen the elusive manuscript, but I had been promised a glimpse today.

"So what are you doing? Sitting on your ass and drinking piña coladas?"

"Actually, Maalox."

"What?"

"The food. I e-mailed you. I eat Mexican food and Tums all day long. I can't take it. Do you know Roland Riggs will not leave his house from seven o'clock to eight o'clock each night?"

"Why?"

"*The Wheel* and *Jeopardy.*"

"I like *Jeopardy.* Nothing wrong with that. Alex Trebek is a smart guy."

"*The Wheel? The Wheel,* Lou. The man whose command of the English language has sent high school seniors scurrying for *Cliffs Notes* sits on his couch with his housekeeper each night and tries to guess nine-letter words for occupations beginning with 'a.'"

"Architect."

"Hmm?"

"A nine-letter occupation beginning with—"

"I got it.... Look, what if he doesn't have it anymore?"

"How bad can it be? You can whip it into shape. Remember Tawny Phelps."

"How can I forget? The woman who composed her book on cocktail napkins where she scribbled the bedroom secrets of Washington, D.C."

"But you turned it into a modest seller."

"And then she left us for deeper pockets. And her next book sucked."

"Because she didn't have you."

"Okay. I'll fix Riggs's book no matter how bad it is."

"And maybe it's great. Now how are you, really?"

I heard the trepidation in his voice.

"I know about my mother, Lou. Stratford Oaks called here."

"She's a bitch, Cassie. I'll give her that. But don't let her make you crazy."

"I already am crazy. I will spend his entire estate on his

care. There'll be nothing left. Did I tell you I bought them a new van?"

"Stratford Oaks?"

"Mmm-hmm. And I paid for new eyeglasses for three of the residents who couldn't afford them. Anonymously of course."

"You're insane. Literally. What is she entitled to? Fifteen percent or something? You're gonna screw yourself out of your father's money—which you know he wants you to have—in order to screw your mother?"

"Precisely."

"You are the most stubborn—"

"I know. Gotta go, Lou. Kisses. Hugs. Love you!"

I hung up and decided to venture downstairs. I had bypassed whatever Maria's breakfast had been by sleeping in. I would drive to 7-Eleven and eat a pack of Twinkies before I would put another breakfast burrito in my mouth.

Maria, as expected, was whipping up something red for lunch. Very red with tomatoes and chili powder.

"Hungry?"

"No. I'm going to run to the store. And then I think Roland and I are going to do some work on his book finally."

"He's the smartest man I ever met. And the nicest."

I watched as she added ingredients in pinches and dashes, no recipe, just a familiarity with the kitchen that I would never know. A Mexican Julia Child in a curvaceous body with a knockout smile.

She sighed and started rolling out dough on a pastry board.

"He takes me out to the nicest restaurant on Sanibel every year...on June 22."

"Your birthday?"

"No, the anniversary of the day I started working for him. But he never forgets my birthday either.... And you see that stove?"

I nodded.

"Jenn-Air. When the old stove broke, he actually took me to the store and let me pick the very best one I wanted. The very best stove."

"That's nice," I said, not knowing a Jenn-Air from a dishwasher myself.

"I never had the best. Not of anything. And now I have the best of everything. And he says no matter what happens—even if he—knock on wood—" and then she crossed herself three times "—I can live here until I die."

"That's very nice of him. You can take care of all his animals."

"Actually, Mister Riggs didn't have any pets until I came here. I told him it's no good to have no pets, no plants, no flowers. Nothing living. It makes you want to die. So that is why I feed him life. I grow my own chili peppers out back and make sure the food is very alive. Nothing from a box or a can. Nothing is too good for my Mister Riggs."

Mister Riggs the *Wheel of Fortune* guru. The Pulitzer-prize-winner. The Bee Gees aficionado. The Tums addict who couldn't tell his hot-pepper housekeeper she was killing the both of us.

With that the multifaceted Mister Riggs entered the kitchen.

"No lunch for us today, Maria. We're off to work."

She smiled. "Dinner at 6:30. Your favorite."

Roland Riggs stared at her blankly, as if he could not recall what his favorite was.

"The taco casserole I make."

His reaction was perfectly timed, with a broad smile. "Of course! Splendid."

He took me by the arm and escorted me out the door and into the garden.

"A throat-burner of the highest order. Make sure you're ready tonight."

He walked ahead of me in long strides. Today he wore a T-shirt with Garfield on the front and a pair of Levi's. He stepped over to a garage and lifted the door. Inside sat a Cadillac convertible.

"She's a 1966 beauty. Look at all that chrome."

"She" was painted a deep black-purple and gleamed from end to end. I found out her name was Ethel, and she had once belonged to his late wife.

"Ethel and I go way back. See these fuzzy dice? Maxine won them at a state fair."

I climbed in the front seat. Roland Riggs slowly backed her out into the brilliant Florida sun.

"Ethel…it's time for a bender."

And so Roland Riggs, Ethel, and I headed down Periwinkle Way, in search of beer and Twinkies.

10

"Rollie!" The Tiki bar's bartender, an enormous man in a Hawaiian shirt and Ray-Bans, greeted America's most famous living literary legend with a gleaming smile set against his dark skin.

"Rollie?" I raised an eyebrow as we sat down at a worn picnic table and stared at the waves.

"Pathetic, isn't it? Sounds like a child's toy or something. A Rollie Ball. A Rollie Bear. Doesn't suit me."

"So tell him to call you Roland."

"I thought of that," Roland stared off into the distance, "but he's a man in obvious denial. Perhaps even pathological derangement. He frightens me."

"Why do you say that?"

"Men who weigh 350 pounds should not wear shirts

with large orchids on them in shades of pink so blinding you need sunglasses to take it all in."

I laughed out loud. A waitress in Daisy Duke shorts and a tight T-shirt brought us a bucket of Coronas.

"My usual," Roland explained. "Would you rather have something else? A piña colada or something?"

"Do I seem like the tropical drink type?" I asked, opening a Corona with the accompanying bottle opener. I raised my bottle with a nod at Roland, and took a swig.

"No. But what do you usually drink? Besides the coffee I smell at all hours?"

"Bourbon. Tequila shots."

"My kind of gal. Maxine didn't drink much. But when she did, she always had a whiskey sour. Yes...and we...we always asked for an extra spear of fruit. Then we used to take the little plastic swords and have a sword fight."

I stared at him, aware of the crow's feet and the deep crags that ran down his face. He was still quite handsome, and his eyes were as vivid as a teenager's. But they had the startling intensity that comes from a man who has seen too much in his lifetime. Being old before his time. Yet when he mentioned the sword fight, I saw a young man for a moment. Before all he had seen.

"My father used to drink Manhattans."

"I used to hear about your father. Back when *Simple Simon* came out. They trotted me off to one literary function after another until I finally decided. My rules. No press. No interviews. No signings. The book stands on its own. But your father…I think I could have had a pissing contest with him." He hoisted his beer.

"Sounds like you and Lou had quite a pissing contest in Key West."

"Yup. It's the piss I miss."

"Poetic."

"Thought it would grab ya."

"So tell me about the new book."

"It's a love story."

"Okay."

"Spanning twenty-five years. And two women. And one man."

"A triangle. I like that."

"And it's a poem."

The Corona started giving me heartburn.

"A poem?"

"Yes. A love poem."

"One poem?"

"Sort of in the tradition of Chaucer. Or *Beowulf.* An epic poem."

"I see. Just how *long* is this epic poem?" I asked, as my brain imagined the fiasco of printing a book no one would read but the most die-hard critics and *Simple Simon* fans.

"I think you'll need another beer," he handed me a fresh Corona from our bucket and waited until I opened it. "It's 792 pages."

Full-fledged heartburn burst through my chest like a flame-thrower's torch.

"Do you have any of those Tums?"

"Now don't judge it before you even read it. Drink more."

He handed me the Tums.

"I'm trying to remain calm," I said as I crunched down on the now-familiar fruity chalk. "You know, Roland, I'm developing a major ulcer. When are you going to tell Maria that she's killing us? I can't go back and eat her tamale pie or whatever she's making after a bucket of Coronas and the news that I have just inherited a 792-page poem."

"She makes me vast quantities of food I can't eat, and I feed it to her cats. But it's the... gift of it. How she grows fresh jalapeños and cilantro. I can't tell her that I don't like her gift. It's like... well... do you ever fake it?"

I downed the last of my Corona and reached quickly into the icy bucket for another.

"As in sex? Faking it?"

"Yeah."

I signalled the waitress and called out "Two tequila shots, please." I turned to Roland. "No. Though I gotta tell you, Roland, the last time I had sex with any regularity, I still lived in New York City. Unless you count phone sex."

"Doesn't count, though I'm interested if you tell tales. But my point is, why do women fake it?"

"Laziness. Or the guy is lousy in bed. Or they don't want to hurt his feelings."

His blue eyes narrowed. "Precisely. Give the woman a door prize." He handed me a Corona and suddenly I was a two-fisted beer drinker. My head was starting to have that pounding, underwater feeling.

"It's a gift!"

"Sorry. I'm lost."

"The faked orgasm. A gift. A gift she gives the man. He's tried so she feels she must not reject his gift, so she gives him a gift in return. My eating tamale pies is a giant gastronomical faked orgasm."

"The big O."

"Yes." He surveyed the beach smugly, apparently self-satisfied with his bizarre explanation for his culinary masochistic relationship.

The Tiki bar began playing some cheesy remake of the classic disco hit, "Knock on Wood."

"Let's dance."

"I don't dance. Not really. I mean, I did," I stammered as the beer and the heat conspired to make me feel very sluggish.

"Come on!"

He grabbed my hand and pulled me to my feet. We began swaying in a version of prom dancing—two drunken revelers leaning against each other and stepping from foot to foot. Sort of a shuffle, step, lean two-step.

"Could you teach me to dance? Really dance? Disco style."

"Not now. Not in the heat. And I'd have to down some serious tequila shots. Even then, God, it's been so long since I went clubbing. I'm not sure, Roland."

"You must. Promise me. Tomorrow night. Promise."

"Promise what? That I'll teach you to disco?"

"Precisely."

"Okay. I promise. Now can we sit down?"

We sat and talked and sometimes didn't talk—just fell into a companionable silence. We did shots of tequila, slamming them down with salt and lemon on our hands. We went through another bucket of Coronas until I was blinding drunk. At some point, we got on the subject of Michael Pearton.

"He's very talented," Roland said, between swigs of beer. "Not as good as me in my youth, but fine. Damn fine."

I pulled ice out of the bucket of Coronas and held cubes to my temples. It's not a good sign to be developing a hang-over while you are still drinking.

"He thinks he loves me."

"And?"

"Love is...too complicated for me right now."

"When will it be less complicated?"

"Never."

"Precisely. So perhaps...how do you feel about him?"

"We've never met. We talk on the phone. The phone sex is perfect. Uncomplicated."

"Apparently he finds it complicated."

"He finds it impossible, really. But it's over the phone. It's without body fluids and wet spots on the bed, Roland. It's simple. It's perfect."

"Nothing is perfect. And nothing is forever. The two truths of existence."

I pondered Roland's truths. The afternoon seemed to disappear into a haze of alcohol, like the sun lost in the sky

behind hot steamy clouds. We staggered into standing po-
sitions around 5:30. The 350-pound bartender looked even
larger through droopy eyelids.

"I'll call you a cab, Rollie. Leave Ethel here. We'll get
her home."

Roland tossed him the keys, and I fell asleep on a
barstool until the cab came. Roland tapped me on the
shoulder.

"It's the heat," I mumbled. "I need coffee. I can't drink
this much without coffee. It's yin and yang."

"Smoking and alcohol, perhaps, but coffee?"

"Don't ask. Just get me some."

"Cab's here. If you still want that cup, we'll make some
at home."

We rode back to Roland's house in a beer-bliss state of
inertia.

"You realize I can't eat," I told him.

"You must. You must at least eat a little something or
she'll be angry."

"Who runs that house anyway?"

"Any man who thinks he can live with a woman and
not have his life overrun by her is a damn fool."

Maria was waiting at the door with glasses of some concoction guaranteed to keep a hangover at bay. It tasted like
a combination of garlic, lemon, and strained cabbage juice.
I nearly vomited.

"Dinner's ready."

At the sight and smells of flaming taco pie, I knew I was
entering into a potentially fatal morning after. I ate as

sparingly as I could, while Roland chatted with Maria about what they should try growing next in the garden. They grew kitchen herbs and studied botanical books, they said. Roland was seemingly unfazed by our three buckets of beer. And I couldn't recall him getting up to piss the entire time we were at the Tiki bar. I didn't know whether to be impressed or frightened.

After dinner, I knew I needed to go to my room.

"I'm sorry, gang, but I'll have to pass on *The Wheel* tonight."

"Oh...are you sure, Miss Cassie?" Maria asked, smiling, but her eyes were hostile. Maybe I hadn't noticed during dinner.

"Posh-i-tive." My tongue was thick.

"Well, then, you need my book for bedtime reading." Roland leapt up from the table. He ran upstairs as I trudged up them. At the top landing, he handed me an enormous manuscript.

"Remember, it probably will be easier to take now than in the morning."

"A poem. Lou's gonna have an aneurysm. He'll give birth to a cow on his desk."

"He might like it."

"He might. Then again, Anne Rice might suddenly write about happy gnomes in Denmark. Danielle Steel may suddenly write a treatise about the Cold War. John Grisham may suddenly—"

"I get the picture. Good night, Cassie. I hope you decide that not perfect is okay."

"Hmm?"

"Not perfect. Love is never perfect. But that's what makes it love."

I took the epic poem in my hands and, with a sense of dread coupled with an urge to throw up, I headed for my room. There, I opened the manuscript box and read the first page. With a sudden heave I ran to the bathroom and flung myself at the porcelain goddess. Feeling better, I laid my head down on the cool white tile and tried to think. Thump. Thump. Thump. My brain throbbed. What the hell was I going to tell Lou?

11

"Hello, Ms. Hayes. This is Donald Seale from *Conversations* magazine. You haven't returned any of my phone calls, but I know you're staying with Roland Riggs. I suggest you call me at my hotel. The story I am writing on Riggs could blow the lid off anything you're planning on doing. Perhaps you'll want to comment."

I scribbled down his hotel phone number as I listened to my voice mail. I had a wicked hangover. So wicked, in fact, I probably would have imbibed one of Maria's anti-hangover potions in desperation, but I knew whatever was in it wouldn't stay down. Perhaps that was the idea. Get you to puke up your poisons.

This Seale creep wasn't going to give up. The magazine was a cross between a sleazy tabloid and serious journalism. Lots of movie star photos and glam covers mixed with gossip. Glossy. And Seale sounded like an impossible putz. I'd heard a few tales about him hunting down stories. Calling him while in my present state of nausea made good sense. Perhaps my unparalleled bitchiness and irritation would scare him off. I dialed his room direct.

"Seale here."

"Mr. Seale, I don't believe I've had the displeasure of actually speaking to you. Cassandra Hayes."

"Your reputation precedes you. What a pleasure to speak with you. Listen, I really think you should meet me for a cup of coffee. I have some information on Roland Riggs that might throw a damper on Lou O'Connor's decision to publish Riggs's next book. That *is* why you're staying with him, isn't it? Or is there some torrid love affair I should know about?"

"Yes. We're fucking madly every minute of the day. But is that any of *your* fucking business?"

"Coffee or not, Miss Hayes?"

"Coffee. Just so I can pour it on your lap. Where?"

He gave me the address of his hotel, and I went to the bathroom and slapped on some wine-colored lipstick—God, I thought, even my makeup has something to do with alcohol. Then I took two Tylenol. Then one more for good measure. Chewed three Tums. Downed the rest of my coffee. The breakfast of champions.

I went downstairs.

"Where are you going?" Roland asked me, chipper as could be.

From behind my Ray-Bans I heard a frog in my throat

croak, "Have to meet some reporter for coffee. He wants to know what's going on. Spotted me here. Followed me here. Who knows? One coffee with me, and he'll crawl back under whatever rock he came from."

Roland's eyes registered panic. "What paper is he from?"

"Not a paper. A magazine. Look, Roland, I'll get him to back off until we figure out what we're doing about your poem...um...book."

Roland escorted me to the door. Ten cats sprawled across the steps, blocking my path in a fur-lined calico carpet. Roland started sneezing uncontrollably.

"Allergic. Let me close the door."

Shaking my head, I stepped over a fat striped cat with an enormous belly—kittens?—and made my way to my car.

The Sundial Resort is a rambling complex, complete with a pool bar, which is where I would have preferred to meet Donald Seale. Instead, I found him in the dining room at a back table, motioning for me to join him.

I was prepared to hate him at first sight. I was not prepared for how beautiful he was. His skin was the color of pale chocolate, and his eyes were large, round and very black. There was no discernible difference between his pupils and his irises. Just midnight eyes. I reminded myself that I hate beautiful people on principle and sat down, ignoring his proffered hand.

"First of all," I opened, "anything I say is off the record. If you use anything I say, I will hunt you down and kill you slowly and painfully. I believe in genital mutilation as a matter of principle, Mr. Seale."

"I heard you were a piece of work, but I had no idea..."

"I heard you were a prick. You don't disappoint."

"Listen. I'm here to help you."

"No. Whatever it is you 'have' on Roland Riggs you have because you have betrayed his privacy. He moved here to get away from it all, and now you want to sell your little magazine and that is apparently worth your soul, so whatever it is, I'm not all that interested."

"Roland Riggs is a public figure."

"No. He's a writer."

"Same thing."

"Oh. So are you fair game? Can I go picking through your garbage and find out you wear Trojans—extra small— and jack off to pictures of your grandmother?"

"Are you always this ingratiatingly charming before noon?" He clenched his jaw.

"No. Oh wait...you're not fair game. You're not a real writer. You're a parasite. Sorry."

"Have you thought of a career in stand-up if this publishing thing doesn't work out?" He smiled in an attempt to loosen me up and flashed a perfectly straight set of gleaming white teeth. Clearly he bleached them. I was glad I kept my sunglasses on. The reflection would have blinded me. But I did pause for a moment.

"I made you laugh."

"No. You made me grimace. Or a half-smile. Not a laugh. No truce. Where is the waitress with my coffee?"

"You and Roland tie one on last night?"

"What? You follow us?"

"No. Small island. Your arrival at Riggs's compound stirred interest among the locals."

"How does a guy get into the business of tearing people's lives up for kicks?"

"I wasn't born with a silver spoon in my mouth, Miss Hayes."

"What's that supposed to mean?"

"I didn't go to a fancy college. I didn't go to prep school. I didn't have wealthy parents who sent me for riding lessons. By the way, because I can already see I've succeeded in irritating you again, I'll let you know I've heard this about you through the grapevine. I haven't been spying on you. I will add, however, that whatever your parents spent on charm school should be refunded."

He wore an open-necked Oxford button-down, crisp and starched, and a pair of khakis. I looked down. In my hangover state, I couldn't even remember what I was wearing. Thankfully, I had changed that morning. I wore an A-line black dress. No underpants—not that Seale would ever know. Black ballerina slippers. I instinctively felt my hair. Loose but without any noticeable knots or bedhead matted balls.

"Funny. Actually, I was kicked out of multiple private schools, but most of them had a no-refund clause."

The waitress brought over coffee and a basket of breads.

"Look, if it means anything, honest to God I admire Roland Riggs. I think *Simple Simon* is a masterpiece. He's better than Hemingway or Miller. Better than anyone. Which is why this story is…unbelievable."

"And the story is?"

"Look, I don't want you running back to Riggs with this. But, I might consider backing off if he gave me a one-on-one interview."

"Is that what this is? Leveraging for the interview of a lifetime? You are a sleazy bastard."

"Did you know your left eye twitches ever so imperceptibly when you're angry?"

Donald Seale's gaze held mine, and I felt my blood pressure rise from both anger and something akin to lust, but I forced myself to find physical flaws. His nose was straight and perfect, his neck hair, I noticed when he turned to smile at the waitress when she had brought our coffee, was even clipped clean. Nothing about him was untidy. I hated him.

"Cut to the chase, Mr. Seale."

"Call me Don. And it's a good thing you're sitting down. Roland Riggs is Maria Martin."

If he wanted me to register shock, he was sorely disappointed. Confusion was more like it.

"I beg your pardon?"

"Maria Martin."

"Are you trying to tell me that he's had a sex change?"

"You have no idea who Maria Martin is, do you?"

I shook my head. From an open soft-sided leather briefcase, Don pulled out a romance book. On the front was a beautiful woman with black hair and black eyes. A man in the uniform of the Union Army was kissing the hollow of her throat.

In Indian Summer Moon, *Maria Martin takes you on another journey of unparalleled passion and breathtaking adventure as a beautiful Native American woman and the man she loves battle prejudice and a brewing Indian war. Against a backdrop of...*

"What is this?"

"As romance writers go, Maria Martin is considered one of the best."

"This is crap."

"It's also written by Roland Riggs."

"Impossible."

"Open to page 72. The sentence I want you to read is highlighted."

"She felt confusion swirl around her like a whirl of locusts. Battering against her face, the locusts' wings buzzed his name.... This is what you want me to read?"

"That's lifted almost word for word from *Simple Simon*. Remember the scene where Simon doesn't know whether to stay and fight or run? He talks about the confusion of locusts, remembering the family farm and the locusts dropping from the roof beams and crawling through every crevice. Some of the words...the confusion, the locusts, are identical."

"You call this investigative reporting? So what?"

"Flip through the book, Cassie. All those highlighted words aren't plagiarized per se, but they're phrases the two books have in common. I've spent months poring over the two of them, and I'm convinced it's the same writer."

"So what? This Maria Martin's a copycat. A bad copycat."

"That's what I thought, too. Until I hounded someone at Zephyr Press for the address for Maria Martin. After ten or fifteen phone calls, this woman finally relaxed a little on the phone with me. I can be charming if I want to be, you know."

Again he blinded me with white teeth.

"She told me Maria Martin is an old woman who lives on Sanibel Island. She doesn't do the romance book tours. She doesn't answer fan mail. That's pretty unusual for the romance trade. But her books are very popular anyway. She's the 'queen of unrequited love.'"

"So this Martin lives here, and you think she's Roland Riggs. Arguably the greatest talent who ever lived is really a romance hack—that's your theory? That's what got me out of bed and dressed despite this insufferable hangover? That's *all* you've got? Some similar phrasing?"

"It's not as far-fetched as you think."

"What did you do? Wake up this morning and smoke some particularly strong pot before you called me? This is absurd. You're inventing a mystery that isn't even there. This is like the Beatles and 'Paul is dead.' This is like Elvis being alive. This is bullshit."

"I know I'm right, and when I prove it, I'm going to write the story of the decade. Unless he agrees to an interview with me."

"He'll never do it."

"You could talk to him."

"He has no reason to do it. He's not this Maria Martin."

As I said the word Maria, I faltered for a fraction of a second.

"What?"

"Nothing."

"You know something."

"Look, if you write this story, you will look like journalism's biggest fool. Go ahead. Write it. See if you ever get the respect you stay awake at night craving."

Donald Seale faltered himself. He blinked those dark eyes of his, and I knew I wounded him for a moment. I had guessed the chink in his armor. I hadn't found a physical flaw, but I had found an emotional one.

Standing, I said, "I suggest you leave Sanibel before you make an even bigger ass of yourself."

I grabbed a croissant for the road, shoving it in my purse. I took a swig of coffee.

"If you weren't so intent on being a bitch, you might actually be very beautiful," he whispered.

I stared him down. Then I turned and made my way toward the exit. The restaurant was empty. With my back to him, I lifted my dress and mooned Donald Seale. *Conversations'* hotshot journalist.

"Kiss mine," I muttered and strolled out into the light of the midmorning Florida sun.

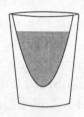

12

"Maria?"

I eyed her as she cooked something so horrific the smell alone made me gag.

"Yes?" She didn't look at me.

"In Mexico... did you ever have locusts?"

"Locusts? *Non comprende.*"

"Bugs. Like flying grasshoppers."

"No. No flying grasshoppers."

"Hmm. Thanks."

I walked upstairs to my bedroom and took out the book I had filched from Donald Seale. He hadn't asked for it back during our conversation, and I had put it in my purse as I stood. Passage after passage was highlighted. I had a copy of *Simple Simon* with me. Donald was right. Key phrases and scenes were shared. In one passage in *Indian Summer Moon*, Maria Martin described her lead character:

Her hair fell halfway down her back, a cascade of black mica, almost liquid, perfect and shining. Her eyes were equally dark, and their effect was hypnotic.

In *Simple Simon*, the lead character visits a whorehouse:

Simon requested an Asian girl, and he was greeted by a young Korean beauty with a shy smile.

"Take your hair down," he whispered. Trying to shut out the jungle, he forced himself to stare at her cascading hair, black liquid mica, perfect, shining. He was safe, he told himself. Breathing deeply, he turned her face to look at him, wanting to get lost in her eyes, dark black pools, pupils indistinguishable from irises, hypnotic and soothing at the same time. No fire, no gunshots. Just this one girl offering herself to him.

I turned pages in both books, flipping back and forth. I tried to tell myself Donald wasn't onto anything. But I knew he was. But was it that Roland Riggs wrote romances when he wasn't writing lengthy and commercially suicidal epic poems? Or was it that his housekeeper was a plagiarist? Or someone else who lived on the island? Or something else entirely? My head hurt. I decided to log on to my e-mail.

Cassie:

You took my highlighted copy of *Indian Summer Moon*. While I suppose I might like to pretend you did this because you want to see me again and this makes a fine excuse, the view of your lovely and pert derriere as you left the restaurant perhaps tells me otherwise. Please call me at my hotel, though, because I really need my copy back. And please consider my offer to back off the story if Roland Riggs will agree to an interview. He is Maria Martin. I feel it in my bones.

Donald

P.S. I don't think I have ever been so angry and so amused by a woman in many years. Not since Patty Maloney tried to stab me with safety scissors in third grade and then told me she loved me.

In retrospect, perhaps mooning Donald Seale was not the best exit I could have chosen.

Donald:

I will call you soon to return your book. You are clearly mistaken...he is most definitely not Maria Martin. You, however, deserve to be stabbed with safety scissors. Apparently Patty Maloney didn't teach you much.

Cassie

My next e-mail was from Lou. Lou is a notoriously horrible typist. He has an excellent assistant who edits all his letters, but his e-mails are full of errors.

Cassie:

What the hell is up with the bok. You promisd me you were going to call as soon as yu looked at it. Areyu trying to kill me or something?

Lou

Dear Lou:

I am not ready to talk about the book with you yet because I am not done reading it. Let me say, though, that it is more imperative than ever that you keep your mouth shut about Roland Riggs because I am not sure if this is as marketable as *Simple Simon*. Will call soonish. Promise.

Cass

Next e-mail...more hell from Kathleen, my author with photo envy.

Cassie:

I understand I am now getting a full back cover photo. But now I really am having second thoughts about my head shot. I think it maybe makes my face look a tad puffy. I am going to have them reshot. Please put the back cover on hold for just a few days.

Kathy

Kathleen:

I think you would be crazy to reshoot the pictures. Everyone thinks you look like a young Kathleen Turner...from her *Body Heat* days. There is no way you could take a better photo. Honest. Don't delay the book. The head shot is beyond perfect. All the men in the office are drooling over it.

Cassie

Actually, I have seen better pictures of Kathleen. However, she is such an annoying pain in the ass, I rather liked the idea of puffy pictures.

Of course, I had an e-mail from Michael. I stood and walked around my room, delaying the agony of opening it. I wasn't sure where he and I were headed. I felt my heart skip a beat for a fraction of a second every time I had mail from him. But if my first marriage didn't teach me anything about how absolutely horrible I am in a relationship, then I deserved to be stabbed with safety scissors. I ate two Tums and then opened the e-mail.

Cassie:

No silliness. No drowning in my cups today. I am just, quite simply, thinking of you. I have this picture of you from a magazine. Lou tells me it's a terrible picture. You're not even facing the camera. But you are laughing with Lou and two authors, and I am filled with both desire and envy. I should be making you laugh. I should be making you cry. I should be making you feel the rhythms and cadences of this dance of life.

I am not sure how this all got so serious, Cassie. But we've talked more than I have ever talked to any woman. All our late nights and dawns and discussions, and e-mails. I've said so much to you, but not the important things. I've avoided telling you about my secrets until now they threaten to get in the way. I am muddling along, trying to decide if being honest is worth risking all the lightness we have and all our talk of your perfect breasts and my 14-inch cock and all our racy late-night musings. Will I throw it all away if the secrets spill out and you won't have me? Because when I see you laughing in the magazine, Cassie, I know I don't have you now anyway. I am willing, I think, to chance it. Let me make you laugh and cry. I promise I will do both. I guarantee it. I'm a stupid ass really, sometimes. I do make women cry. And yet I have even been learning how to make coffee. I bought this silly machine at a Starbucks—they've arrived in London as part of their plan for global domination, you know. And I don't even know if what I have made in this new pot is rot because I don't drink it. It seems to have the consistency and color of black oil or mud. But I am trying.

Should go...it's late and my editor is going to have my bottom if I don't finish this next chapter. She's a real slave driver. But she's brilliant. And I adore her,
Michael

In the quiet of my room, with the scent of jasmine floating up from the garden, mixing with the salt air and fire and sauce of Maria's kitchen, I felt tears—foreign and unwelcome—forming. I couldn't write back. Not yet. Donald Seale, a bad epic poem, Lou O'Connor's financial troubles, my mother's death watch...this ulcer I was developing...and a brilliant man in London were all conspiring to drive me stark raving mad.

13

I confess to you in a velvet box
hushed
fallen
claim my host
tongue pressed forward
claiming you
for me
for all eternity.

Last rites now
anguish
oiled crosses
speaking death
whispering velvet
useless crosses

unfulfilled promises
on the wall.

After death it is
tomatoes, I recall
your own Gethsemane
a garden for us
an Eden now
a wasteland
bloodstained soil
caked in death
ashes to your
ashes
dust to your
dust.

A child now
dancing in my kitchen
amidst potato bonsai
can I learn to
eat vine ripe tomatoes
grow greens
again?

Teach me, Mother Confessor
Teach me, hear me
touch me
let me
go

out of Eden
hell
fallen angel
rage and hate
intermingled with
nothingness
not love
just
life.

I sat reading Roland's poem. No. Lou and I would most definitely not be retiring on its sales. There was a point when, at disastrous moments like this one, I would have visited my father. We shared a passion for writers and books. From the time I was a little girl, I remember books filling every nook of our immense apartment. Galleys spilled off his worn oak desk and tumbled into his chair. When the chair was full, the pages filled the corner of his office. And if not galleys, then crossword puzzles.

"What's a six-letter word beginning with 'a' for a 'large South American rodent'?" I asked, mouth half-full of Cheerios, as I sat doing the *NY Times* Sunday edition. A requirement every Sunday since I turned ten.

"Agouti," he said, absentmindedly, not even having to look up from the manuscript he pored over. His brilliance overwhelmed others. He never forgot a name or a face. He remembered the birthdays not only of his assistants and the mail boys and our housekeeper and the doorman, but also all the birthdays of their children and spouses and

grandmothers. He knew the birthday, I reasoned, expo-
nentially, of every person in the 212 area code.

Where had that mind gone? I remember I had just returned from a trip with Lou to California. Dad called me.
He had lost his keys and needed to change all his locks.
Age, we both said. And then he couldn't find his way home
from Oggi's, his favorite Italian restaurant. And then he forgot Tony the doorman's birthday. And then Tony's wife's
name. And then, one day, my name.

"I'm sick, Cass," he looked up at me, his face stricken
as he both recalled my name and realized something was
profoundly wrong in the same instant.

"I know," I whispered. And I became his Mother Confessor. Roland's poem wasn't far off from my own life.

I moved to Florida because Lou wouldn't have it any
other way. New York was too full of Helen's memories
wafting through their brownstone like a ghost. I went because he asked and also because we all knew someday I
would need to find a place for my father. A beautiful, quiet
place with gentle people who would remind him where
his room was if he needed reminding. And so we came to
a pink little dot on the map, the land of beach bunnies and
buffed bods, and my father went to Stratford Oaks. And
he began to tell me everything he could remember, to tell
me it all before it was lost forever.

My first lost tooth. My first bra (relived with great
humor). His legendary Christmas parties back when he
and my mother were a couple. His lunches at The Four
Seasons and Le Cirque. The time he fought with E.L.

Doctorow. His feud with the editor of *Harper's*. His secret three-day fling with Ava Gardner. His days at Yale. How he wanted me to have all his books and all his possessions. How he wanted to die before he got too bad. I listened to his confessions. The time he almost considered remarrying to Lois Wharton, but he didn't because she never let me mess her hair when I hugged her.

And I would go home after each confessional and collapse. With each story, I felt my insides slipping away with the tide outside my balcony. Slipping away until I was so steeled against the pain, I wasn't sure anything was left. Suddenly, there on Roland Riggs's island, I desperately needed to hear my father's voice.

"Stratford Oaks."

"Please ring Jack Hayes for me."

Four rings, and then his tired voice. "Hello?" So feeble.

"Daddy? It's Cassie," I said slowly, deliberately, loudly.

"Cassie…" I could picture him thinking, trying to place the name, my face. I heard the confusion. And then, thankfully, "Cassie. My daughter. Cassie. Yes, Cassie."

"Daddy, I just want you to know I love you. I'm sorry I haven't been to see you this week, but I'm away. I wasn't sure if you remembered that."

"You haven't been to see me?"

"No, Dad. I've been away."

"Away where?"

"On business, Dad. About a book. A bad book. Not bad, really, just not anything I can publish. Dad?"

"Yes, Cassie?"

"Do you remember the way you used to edit my English papers? And you always made me do them over...but once I did you always gave me an 'A.'"

"I did?"

"Yes, you did. Thank you, Dad. That's all. I better let you go."

"Cassie?" His voice was stronger.

"Hmm?"

"Some books are only meant to speak to the author."

"What do you mean?"

"The author's working something through in his head. And the editor's just an innocent bystander."

"So what do you do?"

"About what?"

"Nothing, Daddy. Nothing. I love you."

"I love you, too, sweetheart."

I hung up the phone. What was Riggs spewing on his pages? And who was Roland Riggs's confessor? Maxine? Maria? Or me? A bystander in a mess of epic proportions.

14

More memories.

"Do you, Cassandra Hayes, take this man to be your lawfully wedded husband?"

Elvis stared at me expectantly. I noticed large sweat stains in the armpit of his sequined jumpsuit. His sideburns dripped with hair dye and Vaseline. I stared at my husband-to-be, the man whom the state of Nevada, city of Las Vegas was less than sixty seconds away from declaring my husband.

"Sure."

Elvis shrugged.

"And do you—" he stumbled over the name "—do you…Johnny Acid take this woman to be your lawfully wedded wife?"

He nodded.

"You have to say 'I do' or 'yes' or something," said Elvis.

"Yeah. Sure."

"Well, then by the powers vested in me by the state of Nevada and Elvis Presley above, I now declare you man and wife. Hit it, Earlene!"

With that, an eighty-year-old organist with a dowager's hump started tapping her foot and plunking down on organ keys. Her senile husband in a pale blue polyester suit threw rice at us and shouted "Happy New Year," and Elvis began to croon "Love Me Tender."

"Go on, kiss the bride," Earlene nodded at us. And with that, Johnny Acid grabbed me close to him and planted one right on my lips. In that instant, I knew I'd made a massive mistake.

I'd married Johnny Acid because my mother hated him. My father, wisely, assumed Johnny was a "phase." But Mother hated him. Hated him so much that she told me she had lost ten pounds since I started dating Johnny and had to double her Valium dosage. This endeared Johnny to me more than diamonds.

It's hard to say, in hindsight, what Mother found most repulsive about him. The fact that he and his band Dog Vomit earned no money and they all slept in a one-room walk-up near St. Mark's Place with a bathroom down the hall and roaches so big you could saddle them up and take 'em for a rodeo ride. His white-bleached Mohawk. That he had pierced his left cheek and wore a dog collar. The leather jacket. The engineer boots with chains.

I told myself I saw past all that. I saw John DeAngelo, nice guy from Brooklyn. I saw him before the name change and spikes and piercings. He was, in fact, a gifted musician and a brilliant poet. His lyrics, if you could get past the screaming guitars and groupies, were art. I told myself I liked his art. But in fact, what I liked was Johnny Acid's cock.

Johnny Acid was endowed. Well-endowed. And he rocked my world. He had a beautiful face beneath that Mohawk. He had a face like an angel Michelangelo would paint. And I believed I loved him. I loved the way he sang as if I was the only one in the room. I loved that he wrote songs for me. I loved the way he moved on stage. He was sex.

I met him at a literary party he crashed with a writer friend of his. We talked. Sparks flew. We made plans for dinner the next night. He came back to my apartment afterwards, and we made love. Only it was fiercer than that. He devoured me. He pulled me to him, *into* him. We pulsed together. It was white-hot fury and lovemaking all rolled into hair-grabbing ecstasy. And after that I was hooked. Johnny Acid was my love drug, and we made love at least three times a day, including quickies on my lunch hour.

Okay. So we were a decidedly odd-looking couple. Me the girl in the velvet dress at the Christmas party, the diamond earrings my father bought me dangling from my lobes. And Johnny, the one with the Christmas ornament hanging from his ear and the T-shirt of Santa Claus flipping the bird that read "FUCK CHRISTMAS."

But I loved him. I thought I did, at least and in direct proportion to how much my mother hated him. The more

Valium she took, the more I called her and regaled her with stories of just where his tattoos were and what they said. I could not have asked for a more beautiful relationship.

And then Johnny asked me to marry him. I was completely shocked, but he showed up at my place with an actual ring. Not a diamond, but a plain gold band engraved with the letters "MPOFYAD," standing for "My Princess Out-Fucks Yours Any Day." A private joke. Guess you had to be there. And I looked at the ring, at dear sweet Johnny. And I heard the word escape my lips.

"Yes."

He grabbed me. We made love. I felt my heart racing, but I told myself it was the orgasm. It was actually something akin to panic.

Vegas was my idea. I figured if I came back and told my father, he'd just nod and go along with it. I was his princess first, after all.

And so, that's how I came to stand before Elvis and make the biggest mistake of my life.

I became Mrs. Acid.

My mother upped her analysis sessions from three times a week to five.

My father drank two stiff martinis and hugged Johnny. He tried to tell himself he'd gained a son.

Lou and Helen sent us a Waterford vase that easily set them back a grand, but said nothing.

And the whole thing was over within three months. I had the marriage annulled. Like it had never happened. Only it had, and I hurt someone. Poor Johnny. He holed himself up in a friend's studio and wrote forty-eight songs about me in a flurry of genius. He dumped Dog Vomit, renamed himself John Dillinger, recorded himself as a solo act, and became famous.

I launched a career.

He still keeps in touch. Calls me from Japan where he's the hottest thing since sumo wrestling. Calls me when he plays New York and gets me backstage passes. I always tell him I can't go. It feels pretty naked to be sung about.

I think about Johnny a lot though. I cannot be trusted. Not with Michael's heart.

It took me thirty-four years to learn that love isn't what's between your legs but what's between your ears. And that brain of Michael's is about the most endowed IQ I've ever come across. And every time I even think about going to England, all I have to do is turn on the radio and hear, "She Killed Me Again," by John Dillinger.

Aka Johnny Acid.

Aka the cock that roared.

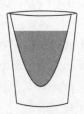

15

Morning dawned. I faintly, in the recesses of my sleep, heard Roland and Maria in the kitchen. I sank deeper into my pillows. Around eleven o'clock I finally felt brave enough to face the Florida sunshine and Louis O'Connor. It was time, I decided, to let Lou know about the poem.

"West Side Publishing…"

"Good morning, Troy. Let me talk to Lou."

"Sure thing."

I waited while a Bach concerto played in my ear.

"Lou O'Connor."

"Miss me?"

"Miss you? I'm ready to kill you. I expected to know page count, cover art, pub date. You're leaving me in the dark."

"Hmm. Well, funny you should mention all that, Lou, because straight up…the book isn't publishable."

"So fix it."

"Well, it's slightly more complicated than that. The best triage in the world can't fix this. It's a poem, Lou. Actually, let me be more exact. It's a 792-page poem."

I heard an exhalation that sounded like the air rushing out of my Bozo the clown balloon when my mother pricked it with a hat pin because she was angry that I wouldn't wear the party dress she picked out for me.

"A...poem?" His voice squeaked. "Cassie, you can't be telling me this."

"You think I should be the only one with an ulcer in all this?"

"Well, you better brace that ulcer for another shock. Cassie, honey? Promise me you won't yell."

"I never make promises I'm not sure I can keep."

"I was so excited about all this—his book—that I kind of offered him an advance."

Now it was my turn to sound like Bozo.

"What does 'kind of' mean?"

"In this instance, it means I did."

"You told me you didn't."

"I figured I'd more than recoup it."

"Please don't tell me how big. I don't think I could take it."

"Big. Very big, Cassie. If this thing falls flat, we could be selling books out of the trunks of our cars."

"Fuck."

"That's kind of what I was thinking."

"Hold on, Lou. I hear something outside my room."

I got up and opened my bedroom door. There sat a rabbit on his haunches, licking his paws and thumping his back foot occasionally. I didn't know whether it was Pedro or José, but he hopped into my room and proceeded to poop on my carpet. How fitting, I thought.

"Lou? Don't you find it a little...corrupt of Roland Riggs to accept a big advance for something he knows can't sell?"

"Maybe he thinks it can."

"He's not that out of it. He may be a hermit, but he's a hermit who watches *Wheel of Fortune* every night. He knows what's going on in the world."

"There's more."

I looked at the poop pellets on the carpet and braced myself.

"I offered a sizable retainer to Tom Gans."

Tom Gans was the tiniest PR agent in New York. He was five-feet, two-inches tall but had the distinction of being the world's biggest sphincter. And he knew PR.

"Lou, not for nothing, but at the time you retained that asshole, we hadn't even seen the manuscript yet."

"A fact I am now quite painfully aware of, thank you."

"I'm going to try to get your advance back."

"But he delivered a manuscript. That's what the contract asks for."

"It's dirty pool. God damn it, José—"

"Who?"

"Never mind. It could be Pedro."

"What's going on?"

"A rabbit's looking at me right now, Lou. Do you hear how ridiculous this all is? Because I hope that thick Irish skull of yours is hearing me. Really hearing what's going on."

"Kid? I got some more bad news. Of a personal nature."

Pedro/José pooped again, as if ordaining my destiny.

"Your mother came by the office looking for you."

I said nothing.

"She looked good. Let me tell you, $100,000 of plastic surgery wears well on her—"

"Sure, but when her skin snaps in two from being pulled back so tightly and her implants implode, I'll be laughing."

"Ahh...the joys of mother-daughter love. Well, listen, I told her I would let you know she came by. Also, I went to see your dad last night. Just to make sure he was okay while you're gone and while that vampire of an ex-wife is prowling around."

My father and Lou were friends. They were passing acquaintances when I was younger, and when I started working for Lou, they had a long talk at a company Christmas party and suddenly, my Dad had a pal. They lunched together regularly, and Dad and I were always part of the O'Connor Christmases and Thanksgivings. When Helen died, my father visited Lou every day for a year and didn't let Lou give up. When my father started getting forgetful, Lou was the one who first made me stop denying what was happening. I remember how he took me out along the beach, and we walked until both of us had exhausted ourselves numb. And then he told me, firmly, that we had to find my father someplace safe, someplace where they would know how to take care of him until the end—because with Alzheimer's the end can be a long way off. Lou helped me find Stratford Oaks. Nothing but the best. But when my Dad really started deteriorating, Lou stopped visiting. I asked him about it once, and Lou started to cry. Not sloppy crying, but just a shuddering of the shoulders. So I had always left it at that.

"You visited him?" I asked softly.

"Yeah. He looked good."

"Did he recognize you?"

"Not at first, but then he remembered a few Christmases and that time you bought him the first-edition copy of *The Glass Blowers*. And the time he and I spent St. Patrick's Day in that pub on 94th."

"I'm glad you went. That means a lot to me, Lou."

"I also gave them a heads up that if they let the rottweiler with implants in to see him, I'll bust some balls."

"Eloquent."

"Another thing…Michael Pearton is telling me that he is completely annoyed that you've gone off to see another author when you won't go to England—and he's done five books with us. So if we're not bankrupt in a couple of months' time, I think you should go and smooth over his ego."

"It's not his ego that he wants smoothed."

"Yeah, well, that part is none of my business."

"Look, Lou, let me get going. I have to talk to Roland Riggs."

"Don't punch him or anything."

"You'll never let me live down that time I decked Carl Gussbaum."

"He didn't know what hit him."

"Right, because he was too busy pinching my ass and trying to cop a feel."

"Call me later."

I hung up and stared at the rabbit. The little furball was trying to eat the cord to my lamp. I tried to shoo him away, figuring frying Roland's rabbit was not the best way to enter negotiations. Finally, I had to lift him. He licked me.

"Don't try to win me over. There's poop on my carpet."

I opened the door and put him out in the hall. The house was silent, except for the squawking parrot downstairs shrieking "Big money, big money," in a voice that sounded remarkably like Pat Sajak's. I figured I'd dress and go hunt for Roland.

In my room, I pulled out my robe and looked at the little picture frame I had placed on the desk. My father and I, many lifetimes ago, it seemed. Me grinning and missing my two front teeth, he in a Brooks Brothers shirt, tie loosened, glasses down at the tip of his nose, laughing at the camera.

I once did a book on voodoo. A high priestess wrote about how to cast spells so that your heart's desire would fall in love with you. While working on the book, I casually asked if she could cast bad spells on people.

"Sure honey, but you don't want to mess with the dark side."

"In fact, I do," I said. I proceeded to tell her about my mother, and she proceeded to give me a surefire spell to make her lose her looks. I had to create a little doll of my mother, using something—material—that had actually belonged to my mother. I rummaged through an old box I had in storage and sure enough found a Hermès scarf that had once been my mother's. I must have borrowed it when I was in high school during one of the rare weekends I saw her. I laughed with delight when I found it, and soon I had a Hermès-clad voodoo doll. I cast my spell. The very next week, a dye job went bad, and my mother lost most of her hair. Her husband bought her an expensive wig and took her to Paris so she could get over the trauma. I put the doll away, certain I would use it again. I still e-mail the voodoo priestess. She has her own Web site—www.cast-yourspell.com. Never know when someone like her will come in handy.

16

I dressed in jeans and a T-shirt and went downstairs to the kitchen. The scent of onions and frying pig fat greeted me.

"Maria? Do you know where Roland is?"

"He left this morning with his fishing pole, so I don't expect him back until the afternoon," she said, her "eees" elongated by her accent.

"I'm going for a walk. If he comes back, please tell him I have to talk to him. It's important."

She nodded, but I noticed her vegetable chopping had gotten decidedly more violent.

"What's the matter?"

"Ever since you came here, Mister Riggs is very upset. He drinks too much. That day you went to the bar...that," she shook her head, "is not good for him. He needs to rest."

"And this," I pointed to a pan full of frying fat and sausage, "is good for him?"

"This is very good. All the people in my family live until 100 years old. And no wrinkles. No. Since you came, he seems not himself. I wish you would get your book and go home."

"Me, too."

"He is a very good man."

"I would like to think so."

"He saved me. My husband was mean...a mean and horrible man, and I was very young. And Mister Riggs saved me. And I just think you come here, and you don't care about him. You just want something."

"And what do you want, Maria?"

She chopped her onions, and I didn't know whether the tears were from emotions or her cooking. "Peace," she whispered. "This is not good. You see."

"You know, I'm not very good at riddles. I'm going for a walk."

I left the house, walking through the garden, and made my way through tall grasses to the sand. I walked angrily, pushing my heels into the sand and leaving little holes as I made my way up the beach toward a lighthouse. I hadn't gone far when I spied a perfect sand dollar amidst a pile of broken pieces. Bending down, I picked it up and marveled that it hadn't a crack in it. I remembered a myth of sand dollars. Inside each sand dollar are pieces shaped like doves. Certain markings on the sand dollar represent Christ's wounds. I flung the sand dollar into the sea and sat down near a dune, feeling tears.

Myths of sand dollars. Myths of Pulitzer-prize winners. Myths of Michael. Myths of me. I dug my fingers into the sand, willing myself not to cry. Myths have no place in my life. I need manuscripts. Pieces of paper that I can mold into a book that will make money. I let the authors tell their myths, and I make them reality. I lay back in the grasses. Love was a myth. Sex was a myth. Family was a myth. My father existed like King Arthur for me. And now he was off to Avalon. A myth. And after he was gone, I would tell stories about him. And maybe no one would believe me. Maybe, after a while, the memories would fade so much I wouldn't believe the myth myself. I remember the time I caught him crying.

It was right after my mother left. In the middle of the night, I heard a sound, and it was him. Crying. Lying on my mother's side of the bed and whispering into the night, "I'm scared." I was afraid to disturb him, yet I ached to see him hurting so much. If my mother went away, and he was hurting, maybe he would go away, too, and leave me with the dreadful housekeeper and her awful German food. I tiptoed next to him and started touching his face, sort of rubbing his cheek, the way he would touch mine whenever I had a fever.

"Please don't cry, Daddy," I whispered. Soon he stopped. I heard his breath come in regular intervals, the deep breathing of sleep, with an occasional shudder because he'd been crying. And then I crept back to my room. The next day, neither of us acknowledged that it had happened. It was a myth. Perhaps it never happened at all. Arthur never had the chink in his armor. He wasn't really off at Avalon.

And Roland Riggs didn't really write a 792-page poem.

I sat up and squinted in the sunlight. Down the beach

I saw a figure sitting in a folding chair. Gray-white pony-tail. I walked towards him, sweating in the Florida heat. Even in October, the days are sweltering.

"Roland?"

"Cassie…I didn't expect you to see daylight."

"Occasionally I foray into the world of the living. What's in your bucket?"

"Bait. Some small fish, a few large shrimp. Not getting any bites today. But I've been watching the osprey. Look at him," he pointed at a huge bird perched high above us on a platform erected on top of what looked like a telephone pole.

"What's with the phone pole?"

"They're trying to lure osprey back by providing places for them to build their nests. Least we can do. We took over the island."

"Roland…why didn't you tell me you took an advance?"

"Didn't see that it was important."

"I can't publish a poem."

"An *epic* poem."

"An epic poem, then. I can't. I want you to give Lou back his advance. Some of it. Part of it. He'll never make a dime on this book, and you'll ruin him."

"You underestimate the reading public."

"What? The reading public? The reading public clamors for sap. Pabulum. Celebrity authors. They're not going to wade through an epic poem, and you know it. In the meantime, you have a very good man…a publisher, staking his reputation on a follow-up book to *Simple Simon* that doesn't exist."

"It exists. It's just not what you want."

"What do you need to publish this book for?"

"I have something to say."

"You haven't said anything for three decades. Why now?"

"You'll see."

"Quit with this mysterious 'I'll see' crap. I *see* a manuscript I can't do a fucking thing with. I *see* that this isn't a follow-up to *Simple Simon*. It's something entirely different."

"I *see* an editor who thinks she knows everything at the tender age of whatever age you are."

"Well, if you crawled out of your island cave long enough to see the world, you'd know this isn't doable."

"I'm not giving back my advance."

"You're being a selfish bastard."

"*You're* disturbing my harmony. I'll see you at dinner. Please…take a walk. It might do you some good." With that, he stared far off into the sea, past me, not seeing me. As if I was a speck of sand in his eye that he could just rub out, blink, and make gone.

"Asshole," I muttered and turned on my heel. I walked far enough up that beach so that he was no more than a tiny dot to me. Then I plunged into the Gulf of Mexico. A week ago, Lou and I had the world at our feet. Today, the myth that I knew what I was doing was washing away with the tide.

17

Pissy. That's how I felt at dinner. That's how I felt after dinner. I retreated to my room and poured myself a large shot of tequila—a highball glass of tequila...straight and neat. I checked my e-mail.

Cassie:
   I really need the book you took from me. And I think we have more to discuss. You know my hotel. Call me.
Donald

Donald:
   I'll call you when I feel I can tolerate a lugubrious, eel-like, bottom-feeding yellow journalist. Right now, I have not had my vaccination.
C.

Pissy. Perhaps pissy was too nice a word. I felt downright homicidal.

Cassie:
I feel stuck in chapter 16. I can't write without your encouragement. What should Sandra do now that her lover has left his wife? Will she consummate their love, at last? Call me and we'll greet the dawn. I'll even promise to behave. To not frighten you with talk of how fond I am of you. I'll be properly English with a stiff upper lip.
Michael

Michael:
Sandra should take a butcher knife to him. The rest of the book can be a homicide investigation.
C.

I drank the tequila, allowing that flushed, slightly drunk feeling to wash over me. I just wanted to escape to sleep. Sleep. Sleep. I poured more. I drank more. And some time in the early evening, I passed out on my bed with the far-off sound of "Big money, big money" drifting up to my room.

I dreamed of Michael. Meeting him and making love to him. I touched his face, and I felt his arms around me rock solid. And then I took a butcher knife to his chest. Tequila does that to me. I woke up with a fog hanging over my brain, filling my mouth with dusty drunkenness. My head was heavy, and I was sweating. My windows were open, and some time in the evening, the breeze had died.

I listened for the sound of the Gulf of Mexico, but it was still.

Pound. Pound. Pound. Decapitating myself was not an option, so I went to my suitcase and fished out some left-over Tylenol with codeine I got when I had my root canal. Popping two, swallowing them with a swig of tequila, I felt sure I could conquer the waves of heat and mid-hangover nausea spilling over me.

Hangovers are bad enough; waking midslumber is worse. Haven't slept enough of it off. The fucking heat. The fucking God damn Florida heat. I looked at the clock radio by my bed. Eleven o'clock at night. I listened to the silence of the house. Roland was apparently in bed or at least in his room. Maria always went to the guest house before ten. I envisioned a solitary swim to fend off the humidity and headache.

I undressed quickly and put on my bathrobe. Sneaking out of my room into the semidark hallway, I listened again. Nothing. I went downstairs and out the door.

Shark bait I do not wish to be. In fact, I can count on two hands the number of times I have actually swum in the ocean beyond my knees. *Jaws* ruined the beach for me. That and sand and heat and obnoxious muscle-bound life-guards and the silicone women who flirt with them.

Roland's pool faced the Gulf. The pool lights weren't on, but the moon was full enough to let me see how beautiful it was. A waterfall cascaded in one corner and Key West-style landscaping lushly filled every inch of available space. Jasmine scented the air. Orchids hung gracefully from trees and flowered in pots. I looked around at the still night, my head relentlessly throbbing. Dropping my robe, I dove in with one single splash and let the slightly cool water engulf me.

Skinny-dipping is the only way to swim. With my mass of black curls, water and humidity are akin to teasing my hair into a bouffant. A few drops of moisture and SWOOSH! Big hair. So if I am going to get it wet, really wet, then it had better be worth it. I had better be naked.

My head was soothed. Coming up for air, I felt revitalized. Not homicidal at all. I did a breaststroke from one end of the pool to the other. I did a handstand. I somersaulted. I even considered calling Michael when I got upstairs. And at that precise moment, I heard Barry Gibb's falsetto. "Stayin' Alive" was floating in the air.

I swam down to the other end of the pool. Leaning my arms on top of the pool edge, yet shielded by the waterfall, I could barely make out the music over the water. But it clearly came from Maria's cottage.

I swam to the opposite corner. Disco. In high school, I liked Zeppelin. I desperately wanted to lose my virginity to Jimmy Page. But I was also a bit of a wild child growing up in Manhattan. I was an underage club kid. I'd snorted coke with a transvestite inside Studio 54. I'd danced on stage at the Palladium. I dressed in glitter, and big hair was an asset in those days. Not a proud moment…skintight Lycra and shiny gold shirt…but I couldn't help myself. When I hear disco, I have to dance. I dove underwater and felt like a mermaid, my hair streaming behind me as I made my way in the darkness to the other side of the pool. Climbing out, I realized I forgot a towel and just put on my robe. It clung to my wet skin. Shaking my hair like a puppy dog, I walked toward the music.

Maria's cottage was quaint. Covered in climbing vines, with cats sprawled on every piece of lawn furniture, it was charming. Her sliding glass doors were open, and through sheer curtains I could see Maria dancing. I felt intrusive and backed up. But it was hard to avert my gaze. She didn't just dance. She *was* the music. She swirled and turned and shook from side to side. She moved like a professional dancer—or at least the best transvestite dancer at Studio 54. She was lithe and moved effortlessly, and her rhythm was perfectly in time with the beat.

But it was more than that. Disco has a rhythm that screams of sex. An endless cha-cha-cha of late-seventies/early-eighties decadence, and she moved in a way that enveloped the pulsating boom, boom, boom of the backbeat. I couldn't help watching. I couldn't help being jealous. She could dance and twist her body in ways that other people, upon seeing her, could only hope to learn to do and never would. Hell…she had *dance fever.*

Closing my mouth, which had somehow fallen agape, I walked backwards, retreating and watching her. And then I tripped over Roland Riggs.

I was too startled to yell. Instead I let out a rush of air, a gasp, and I jumped near out of my skin.

"Jesus Christ, Roland, what the hell are you doing here?" I whispered.

"She's beautiful, isn't she?" he said as he resettled himself on the lawn, cross-legged, and watched her dance as if I hadn't just nearly landed in his lap and interrupted his reverie.

"Isn't this a little sick? You staring at her through her curtains? Let's go inside."

"I can't."

"Whatdaya mean, 'you can't'?"

"It's what I do every night at this time. She dances, and I can't help myself."

"She's a wonderful dancer, who would, I am sure, be really *freaked out* if she knew you were spying on her. This is voyeurism. Let's go."

I looked at him looking at her, and in an instant, I realized why it was he ate her food. Why it was he allowed all these cats when he had allergies. Why the man ignored potato bonsai growing over all his available counter space. Why he had bunnies that pooped on his green carpets.

"Christ... How long have you been in love with her?"

"So long, I can't remember."

I sat down on the grass next to him.

"As long as I've been breathing, it seems. Since I met her, I think. But she was just a kid back then. And she's still... young. And I, my dear, am growing old. I am exiting this world as she is in the midst of its dance."

"Age doesn't matter. It's all in the mind. If you love her..."

"Don't finish that. I can't. But I thought that maybe... maybe you could teach me to dance."

"I don't dance."

"You said you knew the Bee Gees that first day you came here."

"Roland, Maria dances. I just move around like a boob. She has Latin rhythm. That's no myth. She can *be* the music. She probably grew up on salsa and mariachi and music pulsating her world. I can only listen to it and hope to react appropriately."

"But you know the hustle."

"Sort of. It's been a while."

"I read the piece you wrote for *Esquire*. On the end of disco. I knew you could help me."

The full force of what he said took my breath away, just as a breeze picked up from the ocean, blowing Maria's curtains gently. She wore a leotard and her hair was loose and down to her waist.

"Is that why I'm here?"

He didn't answer.

"Roland," I said more firmly, "did you choose your publisher based on the fact that his editor once wrote a piece on disco? Lamenting the loss of the free-spirited age. Tell me you didn't pick Lou, pick me, because of that piece."

He sighed.

I felt the nausea of my tequila-induced state rise again. I felt my heart beating wildly in panic and fury. I stared at him. And then, without thinking, I knocked him over and pounded on his chest.

"You fucking bastard! That poem? How can we publish it? What is this all? A joke to you?"

"No joke. My poem is a work of art. And so is the dance. I need you. And West Side needs me."

"Like a hole in our collective head we need you."

I stared at Maria, now fully writhing to Sister Sledge's "We Are Family." I looked at Roland. My head was throbbing with an intensity usually reserved for New Year's Day hangovers.

I had to think. Think while disco pulsed through my brain. I punched Roland in the arm. Hard. "I'll make you a deal. You write me a book I can sell, and I'll teach you to dance."

"Deal."

"Shake on it."

He put out his hand.

"I'm going up to bed. First lesson is tomorrow. We'll have to do it somewhere where she won't hear us."

"We'll wait until she goes to her cottage."

"Okay, Roland."

Walking back to my room in the moonlight, I saw him framed against her cottage. A man in love with a disco queen. All the Tylenol with codeine and tequila in the world wasn't going to fix this mess.

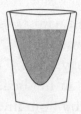

18

I called Michael. Midnight my time put it at dawn his time. Payback's a bitch.

"He–llo?" His groggy voice answered the telephone.

"Greet the dawn with me, Michael."

"Cassie!" I heard the phone drop and him muttering, "Bloody blast it!"

Then…"Are you still there, Cassie?"

"Didn't mean to make you drop the phone. Is it that shocking to hear from me?"

"Yes…I mean no." His voice was a little hoarse. He sounded hungover.

"Rough night last night?"

"You don't know the half of it."

"You must stop bedding all those nubile young women."

"If only that were true."

"Ah-ha! You pretend to pine over me, but what you really want is a nice, young piece of ass."

"What I really want is you, Cassie."

"Please, Michael. Really. It's absurd. We've never even met."

"Then why did you call?"

"I missed you."

"Really?"

I sat on my bed, enveloped in my bathrobe, my skin nearly dry from my swim, my hair damp, and thought for a moment. I had missed him. Missed his voice and missed talking to him.

"Yes. Sort of. I miss the old Michael. Your twin. The Michael of just a short time ago, prior to getting this stupid idea that we should meet."

"Is it really so stupid? Cassie, love of my life, what I fail to understand is how you can think meeting will ruin everything."

"Did I ever tell you the story of my first marriage?"

"No."

"Suffice it to say, Michael, that I am not bred for captivity. I am decidedly... what is the word I'm looking for?"

"Difficult."

"Yes."

"Moody."

"Yes."

"Foul-mouthed."

"At times."

"Hostile."

"Keep going."

"Ill-tempered."

"Yes, that too."

"Sloppy."

"I've told you about my bathroom then. My last cleaning lady was a lovely woman from Guatemala who quit after one day with my mold-covered tiles."

"Impossibly bright, which makes you smug."

"Yes. I suppose that, too. Now, let's look at the logic of all this, Michael. You claim you want to meet me. That you are falling in the L-word with me, and yet you can rattle off a sizeable list of very major flaws. Huge flaws. Fatal flaws. I am hardly the type of girl you want to bring home to mother."

"My mother is dead."

"Sorry."

"It's been years. And you're impossibly right, as always—which, I may add is another reason I adore you—she couldn't have handled you. A Yank *and* a bitch. Or perhaps they go hand in hand."

"Oh sure, start with the Yank jokes."

"Cassie…" his voice grew very soft. "Are you falling in love with this mystery author?"

"No. But I do have to dance with him."

"What?" I heard a flash of anger in his voice.

"Long story."

"Well, I'm listening. You've gotten me bloody up this early when I had a terrible night last night, and you can tell me this long story. Dancing? Dancing? What's next,

Cassie? A tango one minute—and we all know what they say about the tango—"

"It's disco, actually."

"A discotheque? Exactly what kind of working relationship is this?"

"As complex as ours, Michael, if you must know. And we're not going to a disco. Look . . . it really would take me a week to explain."

"Are you sleeping with him?"

I laughed out loud, though it came out as a sort of cackle. Or maybe a howl.

"What's so funny?"

"Michael . . . I think this hangover you have is making you take leave of your senses."

"I haven't been with a woman in two years."

His statement hung between us—across the Atlantic— for a long moment.

"I haven't. And even that was . . . well, she wasn't you."

Michael Pearton was so handsome that I had not a doubt in my mind he could bed every woman in London if he so chose. And then there is the entire sub-breed of literary whores who dream of bedding famous authors, only down a rung or two from rock stars and movie actors.

"You're scaring me," I whispered.

"Why?"

"Because this sounds like obsession, and I can't be obsessed, Michael. My father was obsessed with my mother, and he was ruined by it. He was broken the rest of his life, and he's broken now with no hope of fixing it."

"I am not your father."

"Well, no. You speak with a British accent for one."

"Stop it!" His voice was harsh.

"What?"

"Stop making this a joke. What about the night we talked six hours. Do you have any idea what my phone bill was? But what we had that night was all about a connection between two minds and two hearts. It wasn't a game to me, Cassie. You've never been a game to me."

I felt my own heart beating against my chest. I pictured my father begging my mother to stay. Begging. It was so…degrading. I spent years trying to erase the night from my memory, but of course, I couldn't.

I snapped, "No, it's not a game. But you're trying to make it something grand, and…and isn't it all about phone sex and lying there naked talking to a woman?"

"For someone so brilliant, you are bloody stupid, Cassie Hayes. So bloody God damn stupid."

I heard a glass crashing against a floor or a wall.

"What was that?" I asked him.

"Nothing. Nothing. Blast it. I've got to go, Cassie."

And he hung up.

I thought of calling back. With all of me, I fought this urge to call him back. To tell him I loved him. It was as if I had a physical battle going on inside of me. Like Jekyll and Hyde, I fought the monster. And I fought against it. Down, Devil. Down. And stay there. Stay deep. My monster had a name. I called my monster Love.

19

My mother used to drink gimlets. Does anyone drink them anymore? My father drank red wine. Fine, rich cabernets. He knew about the grapes, the region they were grown in, and he chose his bottles carefully, like a horseman selecting a stallion.

I drink tequila. It's hard and wicked, and a woman who can slam, suck, shoot back a lemon and a glass of tequila is a force to be reckoned with. I drink brandy, too. Hot drinks, with no ice. I drink to forget that my father has forgotten me. I drink to sleep after a caffeine-hyped day. I drink to avoid thinking about how badly I crave Michael.

I woke up the morning after Michael hung up on me with an insatiable hangover. My hangovers all crave one thing. Coca-Cola. The nectar of the gods. It's the only thing to calm the queasies, give me a caffeine lift, and pump sugar to my brain. I massaged my temples and pulled on shorts and a T-shirt before heading to the kitchen.

"CASSIE!" Roland boomed at me.

"Stop talking so loud."

"I'M NOT TALKING LOUD."

"You are, too," I whispered, my mouth full of dry rat hair. I know some people speak of cotton-mouth. That's far too sweet an image for my hangovers. Cotton. Like fluffy clouds. Let's call the dryness in my mouth something *real*. Rat hair. From dead sewer rats. Now we're talking.

"WHATEVER'S THE MATTER WITH YOU?"

I stared at him.

"HANGOVER?"

I nodded.

"JUST THE CURE…" He pulled a can of tomato juice out of the refrigerator. This is a mistake. People think they can chase away a hangover with something that has the thick texture of semen.

"A Coke. All I want is a Coke."

Thank God, he pulled a classic red can out of the fridge, which I proceeded to open and guzzle down with the abandonment of a pirate drinking grog. The phone rang. It pierced through my skull, and I guzzled more Coke. Roland's face again held that peculiar look of a man who never receives phone calls.

"Hello?" he said hesitantly. "Just a moment…" He held out the receiver to me.

The rats were abating, and I found my voice.

"Hello?"

"Cassie, don't hang up."

I recognized the voice of Donald Seale.

"How did you get this number?"

"I'm a tabloid reporter."

"Sorry, I forgot I was dealing with pond scum."

"Listen, I need to see you. I need to see you today. Now. Pronto. There's a new glitch on the Roland Riggs horizon, and if you care about the old guy, I suggest you come to my hotel room. Number 872. Really. I mean it."

I hung up the phone and looked at Roland. Even my eyeballs hurt. "I have to meet someone. Long story. I need to shower... I don't suppose you have another one of these in the fridge."

With genuine concern, Roland pulled another can out and handed it to me. I held my half-drunk one in my right hand and with the left pressed the new can against my temple. I stumbled back upstairs and into the shower. Ordinarily, I am a fan of hot, steamy hour-long showers, but I turned the faucet to cold and suffered. *Wake up, Cassie.*

Remembering that last time I met Donald Seale face-to-face I was hungover, I decided he had something to do with my plight, which made me hate him more. I also recalled that last time I mooned him. Protecting myself against such a moment of insanity, I donned cream-colored satin bikini underpants and dressed in a pair of khaki shorts and a brand-new Ann Taylor T-shirt, strapped on a pair of sandals, brushed my teeth three times, trying to banish the last of the rat hair, and headed out into the heat of the day. My eyes watered from the light, and I quickly put on my Ray-Bans, trying to shield myself from daylight like a creature of the night.

I pulled my banana-mobile out and, Coke can in one hand, CD playing *softly,* I headed toward Donald Seale's hotel. I found his room with no problem and knocked on the door.

"Cassie…" he smiled his mega-watt smile. "Come on in."

I avoided smiling and took a seat on the bed.

"Listen…I shouldn't tell you this, but I like you."

I rolled my eyes, which he could not see behind my Ray-Bans. So I lowered my glasses and rolled my eyes again.

"I do. I really do. So I am doing you a favor. Listen…my paper is owned by Gordon Roth. He also owns the TV production company that produces *Hollywood Now.*"

"I don't watch TV. I take it that's a sleazy show?"

"You might call it that, but it's one of the most popular shows in syndication. They do stories on movie stars, music acts…and authors, if they're big enough or have a scandal attached to themselves."

"I see," I said cautiously.

"Well…they're going to air a show tonight. About Roland. Or, more precisely, about his wife."

"His wife is dead."

"Yes…but she was very glamorous in her heyday, and Roland is a mystery. And they have someone…an old guy dying of pancreatic cancer, who says he's the hunter who shot her. He's going to cry and beg for forgiveness on national TV. He wants to speak to Roland before he dies."

"Have you people no shame?" I was still clutching the Coke can, which I again leaned against my temple. From the Florida heat on the drive over, it had warmed; it wasn't cold enough to help me any.

"I don't work for the show." He looked at me, trying to judge my reaction. He was again impeccably dressed, and I noticed he had his initials embroidered on the pocket of his shirt.

"So what do you want, Donald?"

"I think the show is going to upset Mr. Riggs—"

"I think that's a fucking *understatement*. And who even knows if this asshole is telling the truth. I am, Donald, quite fucking sick of you and your sleazoid tactics."

"All I'm asking for is an interview. I asked you to come here so maybe you could brace the old guy so it isn't such a shock to him. I asked you to meet me here in all sincerity to do you a favor."

"So long as I do one back."

"You're so beautiful, Cassie. And you never smile."

"I do. Just not for you."

He kneeled down on the floor in front of me.

"If it makes you feel any better, I don't want to upset him any more than you do. I wish this hunter never turned up...that he'd died with his secret. But then I started thinking that maybe it would help Roland. Maybe it would give him...I don't know...closure. But I want you to know that I read *Simple Simon* fifty times. A hundred times. I wouldn't want to hurt him."

"Have you ever stopped to think that this man...this

man is just an ordinary man who wrote a book? Maybe he was expressing things in his heart. Maybe he had nothing better to do. But he wrote a book, and since then… thirty years ago…everyone and their brother thinks they know him, that they have a right to intrude on him, to find out what the book means on a deeper level. Well, he doesn't owe you that. He doesn't owe anyone that."

"Look, I just wanted you to know about the show." With that, Donald leaned up to me and kissed me. After a few seconds of shock, I kissed him back. I thought of dead rat hair in my mouth. Then I thought of how beautiful Donald was. How his skin was the color of coffee the way my father used to take it. I felt my heartbeat quicken. He was here. Michael was there. Michael wasn't even speaking to me, judging by our last conversation. I kissed Donald harder. And then the residual effects of tequila passed through me. They cleared out of my brain, and I remembered just who it was I was kissing. I pulled back. Then I pushed Donald backward and stood up.

"This is crazy."

"You'll never know what it's like to question what it is you're doing, Cassie Hayes. You could have done anything you wanted with your father's connections. You, who used to dine with literary royalty. I do my job. I hope I can get to the top…strike a book deal or two…get out of this business. But you—"

"You haven't the slightest idea of what I question, Donald. You can't imagine what I question every day," I said, as thoughts of my father flashed through my mind. It was

Lou who talked me into placing him in a facility rather than caring for him at home. Lou told me if I tried to change bedpans and hoist him in and out of bed as he forgot me little by little each day, I would crack. I would lose all semblance of balance in my life. Me...balanced. As if that was a real risk.

"I liked kissing you. I've wanted to do that since we met."

"If I fucked you, would you pull back on the story?"

"What?"

"You heard me."

"This isn't about a deal between you and me..."

"Yes it is. That kiss was. Everything is. You came to this island looking for a deal, and you thought I was your broker. Well, you can do whatever the hell you want with your stories, but you won't get any cooperation from me. Or Roland."

"Fine. That doesn't change the fact that I kissed you and want to do it again."

"I'd moon you if I was wearing a dress," I said as I walked toward the door.

"And I'd enjoy it."

I opened the door. "I'd like to think that even if I was born into nothing that I would never become a parasite."

"You'd like to think that, but you'll never know."

"And you'll never know what it's like to earn my respect. So perhaps we're even." I shut his door.

Driving back to Roland's in my banana boat, I thought of the kiss. I replayed it in my mind. His tongue against mine, his hand on my thigh. But thoughts of Michael intruded. And then thoughts of my father... of the first time he failed to recognize me. Thoughts of Roland. Thoughts of disco balls. Lou and the money he'd already sunk into a 792-page poem or whatever the hell it was. Donald Seale was very wrong. Now, more than ever, I knew what it was like to question my every move.

20

"Don't you want to watch?"

"No."

I had found Roland on his pre-*Wheel of Fortune* beach walk, and I told him about the television interview.

"But it could give you closure." I was shocked to hear such psychobabble leave my lips.

"I don't want closure."

"But this man has lived with this all these years and now he wants to—"

"What? Say he's sorry?" Roland's voice held no anger, just a weariness I had never heard before. He faced into the wind again. As the sea air whipped his long gray hair around his face, he reminded me of a Norse king, his eyes the color of the Gulf.

"Not sorry. But just to say what happened. What really

happened that day. Don't you think it's important to know? Then maybe you could really go on. Move on."

"Have you ever thought that perhaps I don't want to?"

"Yes. But there's the whole disco thing. If you didn't want to move on, why'd you ask me here? Why do you watch Maria every night? If not to move on?"

He stood, proudly erect. And then he crumbled, almost in slow motion. He dropped to his knees as ripples of water curled around him.

"If I move on, then Maxine is really dead."

I was silent for a minute, then whispered, "But you've known that, Roland. You've known that a long, long time."

My head no longer pounded from my hangover, but I felt as tired as Roland. Editors are really unlicensed psychologists. I plopped down in the sand next to him and let the warm Gulf water lick my thighs.

"We had no children. And I think about her constantly. Talk to her. If I stop doing that, stop wondering what happened and who did it... then she'll fade away as if she never existed."

"Is that why you wrote it?"

"What?"

"The poem. Your magnum opus. To say to the world, 'She was here.'"

Roland took a shell and tossed it into the water.

"She was here," he whispered. "She was here."

"But if you know what happened... if you could even find it in yourself to confront this guy... she would still have been here. Forgiving him won't make Maxine go away."

Roland stared at me with his piercing blue eyes, crinkling them into a squint. "Might I say that if that isn't the proverbial pot calling the proverbial old coot black…"

"What?"

"Forgiveness? Wasn't it you who said you'd like to do your own mother in?"

"Yes. But she's not on a deathbed asking for forgiveness. She's globe-trotting with husband number five and waiting for my father to kick the bucket so she can come into part of his estate. Not exactly forgivable behavior. Definitely not an accident."

"Cassie…I can't forgive. Neither can Maria. It's as if we live in that house over there and death keeps us company. Even with the birds and rabbits, and bonsai…"

"…and orchids, koi, twenty-three cats at last count, though Lord knows I'm not even sure. I just count 'em in the morning for something to do."

"Yes. Even with all that, we can't shake death from our feet, and that's what binds us."

"How? What is Maria's dark ghost?"

"Can I trust you, Cassandra Hayes?"

"Roland…trust is just so much bullshit. If they tortured me, I'd give up your secrets, but short of that, your story's safe with me."

He dug his hand into the sand of the Gulf of Mexico, pulled up a clump, and allowed it to trickle through his fingers.

"Maria's family worked migrant farms. They were illegals here. And like illegal immigrants everywhere, they were exploited."

He looked at me, perhaps gauging my sympathy.

"The work was brutal. Backbreaking. Blistering. Making fingers bleed and lips crack from thirst. And children as young as five and six were picking fruit you and I buy in the grocery store every day. We don't even think about it. Fruit. Peppers.

"And then along came Chavez. He worked for the rights of the migrants. He toiled for them, and Maria's father joined in the fight—as an organizer, as a leader."

"A daughter of a fighter. I like that." I smiled.

"You're a fighter."

I nodded.

"But this was different. Chavez and her father worked side by side. They were arrested together. They were beaten together. But the sacrifice, the bulk of that sacrifice, was made by Maria's mother and her siblings—all eight of them—as they still worked the fields and tried to make up for their father's absence as he protested and fought and talked to people who could support their cause. They needed the money. Pure and simple. Uncle Sam's capitalist dollars."

The last of the sand had trickled through his fingers, and he picked up another handful.

"If they asked their father not to leave the family, they would toil forever, never breaking free. If he stayed with them, they toil forever anyway. What's the choice? Protest or perish."

"The Prisoner's Dilemma, as they say in philosophy. She...is very beautiful. You can't picture her living in the fields. At least I can't. Not when you see what she's created in that house."

"She's made it a sanctuary for me. She didn't tell me about her family, her childhood, for a couple of years. But I see it now. How it haunts her. It's part of her."

I thought of how my father remained a part of me, how a part of my heart was lost to that heartache.

"Eventually, Chavez won some concessions from the large corporations. He changed things. But by then Maria's father was dying of lung cancer."

I looked down at the sand and found myself imitating him...picking up clumpfuls and letting them fall through my fingers. The sands of time.

"So she escaped. She married the first man who asked. A bastard in every sense of the word. He wasn't poor. He wasn't Mexican.

"She would have been better off in the fields, if her husband had been a good man. But, no, she married a lawyer who was trying to help her become legal. Gain her citizenship."

Roland leaned back in the sand and closed his eyes. "Can you picture what he thought as he first laid eyes on her?"

I shut my eyes to the Gulf breezes and pictured a young and beautiful Maria entering a lawyer's office. My opinion of lawyers was just a step above my opinion of tabloid reporters so my mind filled in the blanks.

"He must have gone crazy," Roland whispered, "seeing

this young woman. Vulnerable. Not able to read. But beautiful. So stunning and Latin and mysterious. And he married her."

"Just like that?"

"Pretty much. But he kept her a prisoner. He wouldn't let her see her family. He wouldn't let her attend her father's funeral. He berated her for her English. For everything about her that wasn't American. And he hit her."

"You know, men like that? I'd like to chop off their testicles and stick them in one of Maria's omelets."

"I like you more and more each day, Miss Hayes."

He picked up a broken shell and looked at it a moment before hurling it down toward the surf.

"There's more, of course. But I'm tired. Suffice it to say, Cassandra Hayes, that there are enough ghosts in that house of mine to haunt this entire island."

"I think you're mistaken, Roland. I think you'd find if you let go, Maria might, too. But you do what you want. Watch the show…don't watch it. Just don't forget we're having a dance lesson tonight. 'Cause if you think you're getting out of writing me that book, you're fucking with the wrong editor, pal."

"Miss Hayes," Roland looked at me, eyes moist, "I most certainly think I found the right editor. Even if she is a difficult pain in my ass."

I stood up.

"See you tonight, Roland. And just so you know, I'm watching the show."

21

If I was hoping for a sympathetic character, it was like hanging my hope on Jesus. Despite raw knees from leaning on wooden kneelers, I never got a miracle when I was six and my mother left. And Orville Hobart was no primed-for-TV winner. Orville, thin and ill-looking, with a scruffy beard and a few missing teeth, wore an "I'm with Stupid" T-shirt on national television. The fact that no one sat next to him just pointed out that the shirt's arrow should have aimed straight up at his own head.

"Yup. I jes' want to make things right. I lived with the vision o' that poor woman lyin' there all these years."

"But how come you've never come forward until now, Mr. Hobart," the perfectly coiffed female host asked.

Orville shrugged and took out a grubby handkerchief.

"I figured I'd go t' jail. Only now I gots to meet my

Maker. I tried to find Mr. Riggs to make things right somehow, but he's some kinda hermit or somethin' so I didn't have any luck. Which is why I called y'all."

"So if you had to say something to Roland Riggs, what would it be?"

The camera panned in for a close-up of Orville, who, close up, was truly repugnant looking.

"Mr. Riggs, I am very sorry. It was an accident. I was following a buck with six points, and it darted right toward your backyard, and I didn't see Mrs. Riggs standing there until it was too late and she was all...dead."

Right. As opposed to *sort of* dead.

"And I just want you to know that if it makes you feel any better, I've led a miserable life and been unhappy all these years."

Then Orville began crying on national television. Then back to the studio. Two plastic anchors smiling.

"Well, Barbara, that's certainly some story. After all these years to want to make his peace with the famous Roland Riggs. There's not a person in America who didn't read *Simple Simon* in school."

"Or the *Cliffs Notes.*" Jenny smiled plastically. *Yeah. I'm sure Jenny read the Cliffs Notes version.*

"Yes, John." Jenny kept smiling. "But where is Roland Riggs? America's most famous and reclusive author hasn't given an interview in thirty years. Will he hear Orville's plea for forgiveness? We'll keep you posted on all the latest developments as they occur."

What fucking developments? Orville was going to die
without dispensation from Roland, that was for sure.

I walked downstairs where Maria was loading up ten cat
bowls with food. She placed the bowls throughout the garden each night and morning. She was crying. The small
kitchen set was turned to the Orville Channel. All Orville
all the time, as they kept airing commercials about the interview showing again at eleven o'clock that night.

"You saw?"

She nodded. "I feel so bad for Mister Riggs."

"I do, too."

"He and I are alike. I lost everyone, too. Now just the
cats and the rabbits."

"And the birds."

She nodded. "And Mister Riggs. Now I cannot ever
leave him. Now especially."

She stacked all the bowls on a tray and went out the
door to the garden. For a house so near the water, so alive
with sea air, Riggs was right. Death hung around like a bad
bonsai.

22

Two left feet is a cliché for people who step on others' toes on the dance floor. Roland Riggs was such a lummox that I daresay he didn't have feet. He was like an ancient two-toed sloth on the dance floor. The way our first lesson went, I presumed I would in fact be older than he was before I got a workable manuscript out of him.

We had designated our dance lesson to begin at 10:00 on the living room floor. We rearranged furniture, sweating and shooing the odd rabbit or so out of the way. Anyone on the staff at West Side who is jealous of the way I come and go, and perhaps believes I don't deserve the salary I make, should see me moving enormous leather couches while rabbits sniffle at my ankles.

"I selected 'Stayin' Alive,'" Roland said as he placed the CD in the player on the teak bookshelf and pushed at buttons until the song immortalized in *Saturday Night Fever* came on.

"Any particular reason?"

"Because I have utter faith in you that you can transform me into John Travolta."

At that point I hadn't yet seen him dance. "Sure thing, Roland."

I remember being part of the tail end of the disco age. New York City children of privilege waiting in line outside Studio 54, my friends and I dressed outrageously, hoping to be let past the velvet rope. One time, dressed in hot pants, with my hair teased so high it hit the roof of the cab as I climbed out, Steve Rubell himself waved me forward, the crowd parting for me and my girlfriends, appreciative whistles and cat calls following us into the club. Anna and Jennifer snorted coke with transsexuals in the unisex bathroom while I drank enough vodka to drown a Russian sailor. I listened to the Bee Gees in Roland's living room and allowed the music to take me back.

"Okay, Roland, let's work on the Hustle."

I took both his hands in mine. They were cool and dry, old hands covered in age spots, but not yet marred by the swelling of arthritis, those gnarled knuckles of the truly ancient. Shaking my hips from left to right, I urged him to feel the bass in the music.

"That's it." I smiled. "I'm a woman's man, no time to talk..." Barry Gibbs's falsetto wailed in the background as the parrot squawked and rabbits ran for cover beneath the dining room table.

"Okay." I moved closer to him, trying to show him how the Hustle is all about reading your partner, like an old waltz, but simplified. The fancy twirls and stuff we could save for later. Then Roland stepped on my right foot. Hard.

"Ouch!" I screamed along with Robin, Barry, and Maurice.

"Sorry, Cassie. Let me try again."

"Okay, left hip shake, right hip shake, move together with both our hands joined, and OUCH!" My left foot throbbed where his foot had landed on it with the force of a jackhammer.

"Sorry. Sorry. I really don't have a knack for this."

"Didn't you and Maxine ever go dancing?"

"No. We didn't even have a proper wedding, so I was somehow let off the hook."

"Well, let's try again. Come on."

He tried. He really did, with all the grace of a whale floundering in shallow water. Of a walrus blubbering on a cliffside. And I tried to smile and act as if I wasn't frightened half to death that my feet wouldn't fit in any of my shoes the next day.

"Let's try a slower song. Perhaps we're rushing things." I went over to the CD player and switched the track to "How Deep Is Your Love."

"Cassie?"

"Yes, Roland?"

"You'd tell me if I was hopeless wouldn't you?"

I stared at Roland Riggs. The first day I arrived…in fact

in my entire life B.R. (Before Riggs), I would have told him. Mercilessly. I would have said, "Roland, you are an unbearable, clumsy ox, and this is the stupidest idea you have certainly ever entertained. Now go bang your house-keeper, get it out of your system and then write me a damn book I can use."

But my life was now A.R. And After Riggs, I could only think of how I was pushing Michael away and how Roland and Maria needed each other, and how maybe I even needed to believe two people could be happy living with potato bonsai and bunnies, even if there was no decent cof-feehouse on this tiny speck of an island.

"Sure I'd tell you if you were hopeless. You're just a lit-tle to the left of rusty. We'll get you up and dancing Le Freak in no time."

So I danced with Roland until my insteps were so swollen I couldn't put my feet down without grimacing. Four "How Deep Is Your Love," two "Stayin' Alive," and one Gloria Gaynor's "I Will Survive" later, and I was ready for bed.

"Roland...I think that's enough for one night. How about you take the *Saturday Night Fever* CD up to your bedroom and practice? You know, just practice getting into the groove."

"Hokey dokey." He smiled. "I didn't do too badly, did I?"

"No," I whispered through the pain.

"Well, you go on up to bed, Cassie. I'll move the furni-ture back."

I went to the kitchen and whispered loudly, "I'm just grabbing a soda."

I reached into the fridge for a can of Coke, then I quietly opened the freezer and took out two bags of frozen peas. I tucked them under my shirt, shuddering from the cold, and hobbled to the staircase. Roland was huffing and puffing over the furniture.

Safely ensconced in my room, I placed a bag of peas over each of my massacred feet. I put the can of Coke to my head. I thought of the sequel to *Simple Simon*. It would make Lou and me very rich. I thought of how West Side would be wooed by Hollywood for film rights. I thought of all that as the throbbing in my feet continued. It was as if they had a heartbeat. I told myself it was all for the sequel. But in truth, I thought of Maria dancing alone every night in a frenzy, moving and sweating the ghosts of the fields away. It wasn't all for the sequel. The frozen peas started melting and going soft. I wondered if I had also.

23

In the middle of the night, I heard a scream that not only jolted me awake but set all my hair on end. The sound was more than a scream. It was the keening of a man in the throes of grief.

Despite the gift Lou gave me of beautiful pajamas, I was naked with melted bags of peas resting on both my feet. I tried to remember where I was and what I was dreaming and told myself it was a nightmare. But then I heard it again.

"Ahhhhhhhhhhhhhhhhhhhh!" The man's voice was unmistakably Roland's. I flew out of bed, grabbed a T-shirt from the floor and threw it over my head, and rapidly pulled on a pair of jeans from my suitcase, nearly ripping my pubic hair in the zipper in the process.

Rushing out into the hall, I headed toward the screams just as Maria bolted up the stairs.

"It's the television show. I knew this would happen," she shouted, through tears.

"He said he wasn't going to watch it."

"He lied. He loved his wife too much to not watch it."

Maria opened the door to Roland's room, which looked more like a library with a bed in it. Books were stacked everywhere, with a king-sized bed off-center and diagonal in the middle of it all. And there, in the bed, lay Roland with sheets and blankets twisted all the way around him and a bottle of Jack Daniels in his hand.

"Ahhhhhhhhhhhh!" he screamed again.

"What, Roland, what?" I asked, moving toward him as Maria became totally efficient, like a nurse on duty in an emergency room. Her movements were spare, quick, with the grace and weariness of someone who has performed them a thousand times. She untwisted the blankets and took the bottle of alcohol from his hands.

"That idiot! That idiot... If somehow..." and he began weeping like a child. Maria shushed him, putting her lips next to his ear and soothing him as she stroked his hair.

"I'll get you something to drink. Some water. And aspirin. Your head is going to hurt tomorrow, Mister Riggs," she whispered. Then she looked at me. "Talk to him until I get back."

She left the room, and I heard her on the steps moving quickly.

"It was an accident," I said in hushed tones, holding his hand as I sometimes comforted my father when he couldn't recall my name.

"If he had been...noble somehow. Or just not such a dumb-ass redneck. What gods are these? What gods!" He shook his fist at the ceiling. "If it had been..." and his shoulder racked with sobs and his nose started running.

"What?"

"If it had been an accident that I somehow could have accepted. But here was an idiot..." He strived to catch his breath.

"And?"

"And my..." his voice broke. "My Maxine. My angel... was killed by a man I would no sooner trust my parrot to, let alone a gun. It's all so doubly senseless. So pre—" he stumbled over the word "—posterous. So pathetic. So..."

He cried. He wailed. "Ahhhhhhhhhhhhhhhh!" Again, he screamed. His gray hair was splayed across the pillows like some eighteenth-century genius in the throes of the plague. Only Roland's plague wasn't carried by a rat, but by a mistake, borne on the shoulders of an idiot now nearing his own last breath on earth.

I squeezed his hand and thought about it. Would I rather my wife killed by an intelligent man who made a grievous error or an imbecile who simply fucked up without thinking? A brilliant life snuffed out by a stupid one. Where was the score evened with that one? Roland was right. What gods? What gods!

Maria crisply reentered the bedroom, her shoulders stiff with total authority.

"Drink," she commanded, and he sat up and took a sip of water.

"Tongue," she commanded and he stuck out his tongue while she placed two aspirin on it.

"Drink," she said sternly as he sipped the water again.

"Lie down."

He did as he was told.

"The bed is spinning."

"Just lie there. Only sleep can cure this."

With that she began to sing a lullaby in Spanish. It was a vague tune, the type mothers make up on the spot for their young children—in any language—to chase away monsters and boogeymen. I didn't understand a word of it, but she stroked Roland's head and held his hand. He sniffled and sighed and eventually fell back to sleep.

"Sometimes death makes no sense, Mister Riggs," she whispered. When she seemed confident that he was soundly dreaming and not agitated any longer, she whispered, "Let's go. He will sleep and maybe dream."

In the hallway she turned to me, "The dead have a way of haunting the living."

"Is he like this often?"

She stared at me, knowingly. "He will never let go of Mrs. Riggs. And the man on the television just reminded him all over again. She is still here." Maria stared up at the darkened ceiling. "She will not let him rest."

"That's bullshit. He needs to find a way to make this end. Death is death. The end."

"That cannot be," she whispered and crossed herself.

24

The next day, I hobbled downstairs to the kitchen. Maria was chopping onions for yet another fatal dish.

"What happened to you?" she asked, the knife hitting the cutting board with a pounding sound. In all the commotion, I don't think she noticed my swollen feet the night before. And I had run to Roland's room so quickly, adrenaline pumping, I hadn't noticed either, but there they were, fat and pink and swollen.

"Oh...I went walking on the beach last night, and I think my feet were attacked by crabs."

"I've never heard of that."

"Happens all the time. You ever go walking the beach at night?"

She shook her head, now dicing the onions into tiny squares.

"Well, I'm here to warn you. Very dangerous."

Maria stopped her chopping and looked up.

"I don't believe you. I think you're making fun of me."

I shrugged. "Fine. Don't. Just don't blame me if the crabs attack your feet. They travel sideways, you know. Guerrilla attack. Stealthy."

I made my way to the door.

"Where are you going?"

"Out."

"What should I tell Mr. Riggs if he asks when you'll be back?"

"Later."

"Today he will be very sad. Maybe you should stay."

"Maria, I'm his editor. You're his nurse and his keeper and his cook and botanist. I would even go so far as to say you're his muse."

"His what?"

"Nothing."

I walked out the front door, taking care to not let in the orange-striped fat cat that was sitting on the doormat. The cat lazily licked his front right paw. Walking to my car, cats slunk up to me and rubbed against my bare legs. Others stretched out by the koi pond and fountain. Still others slept on tree branches, a lone paw or tail dangling over the side. I wondered if the cats ever eyed the rabbits and thought "dinner." I wasn't sure why, but the thought of Pedro or José ending up as cat food worried me. And the fact that I was worried about bunnies told me I had already spent too long on this island.

Driving to Donald Seale's hotel, I thought of the last time he had kissed me. I wasn't sure why I hated him so much, or if I really did hate him. He was just trying to do his job. I told myself that. Repeated it in my head a hundred times as I drove. But when I walked up to his hotel room, and he opened the door, I still shot him down for all it was worth.

"Here's your book." I walked in and tossed it on the bed. "You've proved nothing. Roland Riggs does not write romances."

"I'm still going with the story."

"Suit yourself," I said flatly. How can you trust a man who doesn't even leave wet towels lying on his hotel room floor? He was too neat, smelled too clean when I was near him. Was too good-looking.

"You'll look like a fool when we issue a denial," I said.

"Did you see the segment with the dying hunter?"

"The 'I'm with Stupid' guy? I saw it. Roland didn't watch. You're not going to get an interview. He doesn't care, Donald. It's all in the past," I bluffed. "You're pursuing the Holy Grail of journalism, and I can't blame you, but it's not going to happen. Not now. Not when his new book comes out."

"Can I quote you on that?"

"Donald, I returned your book. All your yellow highlighted paragraphs don't show they're the same writer. It just shows you were the nerd in high school who used highlighters. I'm leaving. When the book comes out, I'll be sure to send you a press kit like everyone else."

"I don't want to wait that long to hear from you."

Even as he said that, he was walking toward me, then standing behind me, kissing my neck. Shivers ran up and down my spine, and, for what it's worth, I wanted to push him away. Instead I turned around and kissed him back. He moaned.

"You make me crazy."

"A lot of men tell me that. Not in a good way."

"No...this *is* in a good way. And the bad way."

I plead amnesia. My shirt was off, his pants were halfway down to his knees. I wasn't sure if I had done that or he had, but the next thing I knew we were in bed, fucking our brains out. He was beautiful. He was a skilled lover. And when it was all over, I was dressing faster than a hooker on the clock.

"Don't go. Spend the afternoon with me. Cassie, please."

"I can't."

"What if I said I'd drop the story?"

"That's not why I fucked you."

"I know."

"There's a spark between us, Donald. You infuriate me and piss me off, and I do the same to you. But I have to go. This was just one of those things."

"Not to me."

"Donald, this was one of those things to me. Here's a little secret about me. A slice of vulnerability that you can tuck away in your Rolodex— My life is one of those things. Some people are like that, Donald. My life...at every turn...is one of those things."

Erica Orloff

I watched him fall back on his pillow and shut his eyes
as I left. When I got to my car, I slid in and started to drive
back to Roland's. I passed the public beach and the lighthouse, and then I had to pull over and throw up. Acid
burned my chest and throat as I emptied my stomach of
last night's booze. But it wasn't a hangover—for a change.
It wasn't the senseless fucking. I had done that in Studio 54's
bathroom. I had done that on my kitchen table. I had
done that behind the Greek mythology stacks in the New
York City public library. I climbed back in the car and
drove to Roland's. He and Maria were eating something
that smelled dangerously like pure chili peppers. I waved
hello and went to my room. The rabbits followed me.

No. It wasn't the fucking. It was that it was Donald and
not Michael. The acid rose in my throat again, and I went
to the bathroom and kissed the porcelain goddess. My nose
was running. My eyes were watering. Believe me, I could
make a case that I am my most unattractive immediately
post-vomit. Even worse than my puffy menstrual days, and
most decidedly worse even than a head cold. I wiped my
eyes. Jesus Christ, it wasn't the throwing up that was making my eyes run. I felt my stomach heave with the real-
ization that I was crying. But I couldn't stop them. The
tears came no matter how much I willed them away.

I took out my laptop and wrote Michael an e-mail:

Michael:
    I've messed this up totally. Totally. I've pushed and pushed
and now you've gone and hung up on me. What are you think-

ing? Are you thinking I'm impossible? Insane? That we were just dancing and now the music's stopped? You're right, you know. That night on the phone. I never used your tea set. Not once. I knew the minute I opened the box I would never attempt to serve high tea, and it was the most impossibly impractical gift I had ever received. I took it out of the box when it arrived and put it on my counter where it sits, gathering dust. It needs to be polished. It's really an unattractive tarnished gray-brown. But, besides the fact that the thought of buying silver polish is completely against my very genetics, I refuse to polish it.

Why?

I ask myself this. Why? It's just a tea set. My cleaning lady threatens to clean it every two weeks.

And I never realized it, until maybe a few weeks ago. But I never polish it because your hand was the last that touched it. You put it in the box and shipped it to America, and somehow I can't bear to buff away your touch. Your fingerprints that linger on it.

The tea set, Michael, looks, as you'd say, "bloody awful." But it's all I have of you.

I'm not sure if this is how someone says "I love you." I've never tried.

Am I crazy, Michael?

Cassie

There it was. My finger poised the cursor over Send. I waited. I read and re-read. I waited. My hand cramped from holding the mouse for so long. The acid in my throat kept burning me. The two rabbits stood on their haunches and looked at me. Expectantly.

"I know, you two. I know."

And then, I pressed Send.

Too late to change my mind. The message was gone.

I turned off my laptop. That was that. I wiped my eyes again. I needed to shower. I needed to wash away my morning with Donald. I needed to start fresh. But first, I needed to finish crying.

25

Late that afternoon, long after my shower, after my nap in which I tried to sleep away my regret, I turned on my computer again and ignored seven e-mails from Donald and waited for one from Michael, which never came.

Cassie:
   I cannot stop thinking about you. I've abandoned the story. I want us to have a fair chance on even ground. Please let me see you again.
Donald

Cassie:
   Admit the chemistry between us is there.
Donald

Donald was going to make my post-coital self-loathing even more difficult. Yet another reason to hate him. Each e-mail urged me to consider a relationship when the poor guy didn't know I had vomited from the thought of him.

I listened to my voice mail. Authors angry over their PR campaigns. Why couldn't we get them on *Oprah?* Authors angry over editorial changes. Authors upset that their royalty checks were smaller than expected. Returns. Returns. Returns. The way of publishing. A bookstore stocks forty copies, sells twenty, sends back twenty—and we have to pay for that return. It's all a numbers game like Hollywood accounting. The voice mail demanded return phone calls, and I couldn't bring myself to speak. Michael did not call.

I went out on the beach and searched for Roland. I found him staring into the surf.

"Are you okay?"

He shrugged. I sat down on the sand next to him. Dusk was descending, and I shivered in the unusual chill. Florida can be like that if the wind comes from the north.

"If it makes you feel any better, I do, in some tiny way, understand. Maybe, in some fucked-up bit of fantasy, it would have been better to have idealized who pulled the trigger. But it was him, Roland. A stupid man with an 'I'm with Stupid' T-shirt—quite fitting, I will add. But maybe it's time to come back to the land of the living. To this island you so adore, despite its lack of a good coffeehouse. To Maria."

"She won't have me. Not after seeing me last night... other nights."

"What do you mean? Seeing you a mess with a bottle of J.D. in your hand? Looking like you're wearing a fright wig?"

"Remind me to ask Lou if you are always so comforting."

"You can count on me, Roland."

"It's hopeless."

"No. Look, I am teaching you to dance, and you are winning her heart and then writing the sequel you owe me. There isn't time for all this wallowing self-pity."

"But I want to wallow."

I sighed. "You also toasted sap when I first arrived. You love her so get off your duff and pull it together, Roland. Maxine is gone. Dead. Shot by a loser. You've put a face to the phantom, but it hasn't changed a thing."

"You're rather…tough on me, don't you think? If you're such an expert on affairs of the heart, what's going on with you and Michael Pearton?"

"He hung up on me. Because I wouldn't agree to come to London. Because I'm here and he's there."

"Because you wouldn't let yourself love him."

"That, too, I suppose."

"What a pair of idiots we are."

"Roland…" I watched a child digging in the sand near his mother. "I couldn't agree with you more."

"Maybe you could talk to Maria. Feel her out about this."

"Feel her out? What is this? Seventh-grade? Sister Margaret Catherine finding my best friend's note to Timothy Hastings, III, in which she was trying to find out if when he launched a spitball into my hair in Latin class he was really trying to say he loved me."

Roland chuckled, and then, for the first time since I sat down, he turned his head to really look at me. "My God, you look awful!"

"Thanks. You *do* have a way with the ladies."

"Good God in heaven, what the hell happened to you?"

"Long story."

"You're pale as a ghost. You look splotchy. Splotchy like you've been . . . I don't know. Just splotchy."

"Again, my ego thanks you."

"It's Michael Pearton, isn't it?"

"Michael and so much more."

"Can you go to London?"

"I don't think so, Roland. I can't fix my own love life. But I'll see if I can meddle in yours without fucking up too badly."

"Thank you."

"I better go talk to Maria."

"And later on tonight?"

"Dance lessons. If my feet can stand it."

"I'll try to conjure up the spirit of Fred Astaire."

"I'll settle for channeling an Arthur Murray instructor. Roland?"

"Hmm?"

"I need to ask you something."

"Sure."

"You haven't by any chance been writing other books all these years, have you? Under a pseudonym?"

He was perfectly still. I looked closely at him, and he didn't even appear to be breathing. Then, almost imperceptibly, he nodded.

"I won't even ask how you got started . . . or why. Remember when Alice fell down the rabbit hole?"

Roland looked up at me quizzically.

"Well, Alice has nothing on my own journey to Wonderland, Roland. You've made sure of that."

"Are you angry?"

"No . . . But I better go before the Mad Hatter arrives."

I turned and headed toward the house. I had thought it was the house that *Simple Simon* built. From its magnificent windows fronting the water, to its gardens of jasmine and orchids, to its deck jutting out toward the Gulf. But apparently romance sells. And Roland was, after all, the "queen" of unrequited romance novels. How those books dwelt within the same man who wrote of war's fury and pathos was a tiny glimpse into just how strange the rabbit hole had become.

26

Maria was feeding the animals when I trudged into the garden, all too aware of my sore feet and the dull pain in my heart. I also felt self-conscious of my splotches. Maria's beauty was always flawless.

"Maria?"

"Yes?" She moved efficiently from one cat bowl to another with a big bag of Cat Chow perched on one hip and a measuring cup for a scoop.

"You certainly are very devoted to these cats."

"They need me. Sometimes Mister Riggs jokes with me that I am feeding all the cats on Sanibel Island. But I know he loves them."

Sure he does, I thought as I bent over to stroke a striped tabby.

"And you take excellent care of Roland. I saw that last

night. You were…much better than I would have been by myself. I didn't know what to do."

"He needs me. After all these years, I just know. It's a gift."

"Is that it?"

"What? My gift? What do you mean?" she asked as she scooped up some more chow and cats meowed and purred at her feet.

"I mean, do you stay because he needs you? Or do you like it here? Do you stay for the cats? What? You could find another job, I'm sure. Go someplace else. See a big city. Leave this island."

"He is my baby. You saw last night…he is like that sometimes. Less now. When I first came, nearly every night. Without me, he would go crazy. I think he would not write anymore. He would just…disappear. And who would cook for him? Who would take care of the gardens? This, I see, is my home. My real home."

"Wouldn't you like to not take care of things? To maybe have someone take care of *you* for a change?"

She paused, mid-scoop, her face thoughtful, a tiny furrow appearing between her brows.

"From the time I was a little girl, I worked the fields. My family moved from place to place. I didn't go to school. I took care of my brothers and sisters. It's more than what I do. More than getting paid to clean a house or to make food. It is who I am. When I came here, he had no gardens. This was all sand. And bit by bit, I worked to make it a paradise. I talk to the plants and make them understand they will be happy here. This is a little bit of heaven."

"But what about dating? Making a family and a house of your own?"

"This is my own." Her eyes opened wide. "Please don't tell Mister Riggs that. It's a way I have of pretending that I am the mistress of this house. I was married once. To a fancy man who knew so much more than me or my family. That's how I met Mister Riggs."

"Really? I guess I never asked.... Do you want me to help you?"

"No. I like doing it."

"So tell me how you met."

"I was here on vacation with my husband. He wanted to go fishing. So we came here from Dallas. See, I have seen a big city. They are not so great." She took the bag of Cat Chow off her hip and picked up a solid black cat and rubbed its face against her own.

"My husband was...oh...when I met him he bought my family many things. Televisions. And a used car. And he...what do they call it? Pro bono. He was a lawyer, and he made a case for us to be citizens."

"Did you love him?"

"I thought I did. But I realized later I wanted to love him to be a good daughter to my family. So life would be less hard." She pulled the cat closer to her. "But life for me was much more harder. He started hitting me. Every time another man looked at me, he said it was my fault. I cannot have any babies, I think. In my stomach he hit me. Very hard. But never my face. That he wanted to be beautiful so when his friends met me he could impress them with his wife."

"But I thought you said if other men looked at you he got violent."

She nodded.

"Well, if that isn't a fucking Catch-22."

She looked at me in the deepening darkness. "That means you can't win," I offered.

"Yes. It's this Catch-22. That is what it was. No win. No happiness. No babies, though I try. So one night, he was fishing all day long, and came home and he was angry because I had a tan, which meant I was out on the beach in a bathing suit. He raised his fist to me, and usually I do nothing, but I screamed. I don't know why. It just came out. And then once I started screaming, it was like I cannot stop. Screaming. Screaming. And he getting madder and madder. And Mister Riggs was walking by our… we rented a cottage. And he just came through the door, and he was like a madman. He took one look around and grabbed a chair. He beat my husband with it. Broke his nose and his arm. It was a very big mess. Blood everywhere. And that night I moved in with Mister Riggs and have never left."

"But what happened to your husband?"

"I don't know."

"Did he go to the police?"

"I don't think so. Or maybe he say he doesn't know who did it. Maybe he was dead. I don't know. We left him on the floor."

"And that was it? You just moved into Roland's house?"

She nodded. Her eyes were very dark. I couldn't see if she was crying. Her face was in the shadows.

"I am here because if I did not have Mister Riggs to take care of, then there would be no reason for me to not be able to have a baby—it would be so much worse. Somehow it makes sense for me to be here. As if I...it was like my father working to help our people. If there was not a reason that was bigger than us all then we could not have beared it. We all need a reason for going on. Mister Riggs is mine. He is the reason I suffered. He is my baby. And the cats. And the rabbits. And the garden. Otherwise it would make no sense."

"It makes no sense anyway, Maria. I hope he was dead on the floor."

"I never even speak his name. And in this garden, I almost forget. He is just a ghost here, and I chase him away with each flower."

"I'm so sorry."

I turned my back on her as she murmured to the cats. Maxine had died in a garden, and Maria lived through one. But as the wind whispered behind me, I was certain the garden had more ghosts than weeds.

27

For the next two nights, we practiced, faithfully. To no avail. Roland wasn't channeling Fred Astaire, and I was weary with the knowledge that this house Roland built with Maria was erected on the shifting sands of a wife beater and the ghosts of babies not to be. That third night, however, I began to feel hopeful that Roland Riggs might actually defy the adage that white men can neither execute a perfect jump shot nor dance. He was no John Travolta, but he was getting the hang of it. Hope glimmered, in fact, that I might return to the world of the living: coffee beaneries and bagel shops, bars that stocked my brand of tequila and cognac. Hope blasted through the speakers of Roland's stereo system.

"I want to learn something fancy," he said, as he spun me, Sister Sledge singing out in the background.

"You're not ready for fancy," I said. "You're a step above walking, but you're getting there."

"How about a dip?"

"A dip? I don't think so, Roland."

"But a dip would really impress Maria, wouldn't it? It's tango-like. Sexy."

"Roland, I—" but before I could sputter off another argument, he dipped me.

"Not bad," I said, amazed he so gracefully leaned me backwards. "Now let me up before my back breaks."

He did, and we continued doing the Hustle. "Another dip?" He laughed, looking positively giddy that he, Roland Riggs, Pulitzer-prize winner, could do the *Saturday Night Fever* "point," complete with hip gyrations. I was ready to buy him a white polyester suit.

"Sure, Roland." The rabbits even looked impressed as they lay flopped on their sides near the couch. I envisioned him and Maria dancing the night away, perhaps putting their respective pasts behind them, and me rewarded with a new manuscript flying off his word processor in no time.

He dipped me. And then, just as suddenly, he dropped me on the floor with a heavy thud.

"Jesus Christ, Roland! What the fuck are you doing?" Pain shot up from my ass and assaulted my neck.

He was staring stock still, frozen. Petrified. From my crumbled position on the hard wooden floor, I turned my neck ever so slightly and painfully and saw, to my equal horror, Maria standing in the kitchen doorway.

"I forgot to feed Julio."

I looked at Roland and mouthed "Julio?"

He whispered, "A feral cat that comes by."

Maria's eyes were filled with tears of betrayal, and Roland's were filled with tears of what was now as ruined and crumpled as our last dip.

"I can explain," he said.

"Don't bother, Mister Riggs. I don't need any stories from you. You owe me nothing." She turned on her heels and ran from the house.

He seemed to have forgotten I was even there.

"Roland? Could you help me up?"

"I knew it," he whispered as he lent me a hand. "I'm doomed."

"Give me a break. Doomed?"

"I am."

"Go after her."

"What? I can't."

"For all your talk of love, you're as scared of rejection as a sixteen-year-old pimple-faced geek before the prom. Go after her," I implored. "Go after her and offer your dance. Let her see it was all about her."

It was clear, from the defeated look on his face, that he was not going to move. So I grabbed his arm. "I need a book from you, and if this is the only way I'm going to get it.... Editor, nursemaid, matchmaker, psychiatrist, how many more fucking hats do I have to wear?"

I tugged him along by his turquoise Hawaiian shirt, half dragging, half pulling, half pushing him to the guest cottage. I banged on the door.

"Maria!" I screamed, "Maria! Look, I need five minutes

of your time, because I am leaving. And sooner or later, I know you'll come out to feed the cats in the morning. So we can do this now or do this in the morning. But I'm tired as hell, and I would rather do it without staying up all night."

She didn't immediately answer, but I sensed we were being watched from behind the curtains. Eventually, I heard her fiddling with the locks.

When she opened the door, I was stunned by how angelic she looked. She was wearing a very long white T-shirt and her hair, instead of being in a single thick braid, was brushed out and full and wavy. Her eyes were puffy from crying, but in the moonlight, her skin was smooth and luminescent.

"Tell her, Roland." I turned to him.

He stood stock still, his lips moving but no sound coming out.

"Tell her!" I poked my elbow into his ribs.

"Maria, I…I wanted to learn to dance for you."

"Please," she waved her hand. "No lies. I'll leave in the morning. I don't want to…be in the way of the new mistress of the house."

"You two are driving me fucking insane!" I screamed. I finally hit my breaking point. Maria's eyes blinked twice, as if I'd verbally slapped her. They both stared at me.

"Floating around that house full of ghosts, wanting each other but never saying it. You," I poked Roland in the chest, "still living in a garden in Maine, afraid to let go. And you," I pointed at her, "caring for every creature under the sun but not your own heart. For God's sake, you two need to live again. It's okay, you know. To join the rest of us living and breathing souls."

"How dare you!" Maria said. "You have no idea—"

"I have every idea. Listen, lady, he hates hot food, he's allergic to all your cats, and he doesn't particularly like rabbit crap on his carpets. But he loves you, and that's what this whole dancing stunt was all about. Proving it to you by stepping on *my* feet and dropping me on the floor. I was teaching him to dance, Maria. For you. That's all."

Roland nodded, willing her to believe me.

"And Roland," I faced him, "I'm through with all this. You talk to her. You say what needs saying. And if you hand me a manuscript I can use, fine. If not, I'm outta here tomorrow either way. I've had enough of this island. And now," I massaged my neck, "I think I have whiplash."

I stormed back toward the house. My teeth chattered. For such a temperamental bitch, I always feel a rush after spewing out my anger. First I flush and feel a release, and then I briefly tremble as the release floods my body with endorphins. I breathed deeply and tried to still the shivers.

I reached the deck and turned around. Through the curtains, I saw them dancing. Slowly, cheek to cheek. She was holding on to him, her head buried into his chest, and he kept stroking her hair. They swayed as one, moving to the music I was too far away to hear. Then Roland dipped her—and didn't even drop her. The move was sexy and seductive. Perhaps their ghosts had decided to let them live after all.

28

The next day nothing had changed...and everything had changed. It was as if the sun decided to rise in the west. The world had been turned upside down, spun backwards on its axis, and yet it was still the same sun, burning hot and bright over the Gulf of Mexico.

Maria still cooked a breakfast that would kill mere mortals. This time, it was runny eggs *without* hot sauce. Sure, I had told her the night before that Roland didn't like spicy food, but it was as if now, without the hot sauce, she couldn't prepare something edible. She didn't seem to notice. And neither did he. She served the eggs smiling, in a daze, reeling in love with Roland Riggs. And Roland was worse. He first greeted me with a bear hug and then picked up one of the rabbits and kissed its quivering nose.

As I forced down the eggs, I asked him, or really stated what we both knew, "I'm not going to get that book, am I?"

Roland looked thoughtfully at his fork. "I don't know if I'm ever going to write another word."

"Not even as the queen of unrequited romance novels?"

He let the eggs fall back to the plate and stared at me. "No more romance novels, though they have supported me in the style I've grown accustomed to."

"So what's next?"

"What's next?" he looked toward the kitchen where Maria tended to her potato bonsai. "The rest is all a mystery, Cassie, but when I solve it, you'll be the first to know. And thank. The bigger mystery, of course, is what's your next move?"

"Mine?"

"With Michael Pearton."

"Some mysteries, Roland, are best left unsolved. I wrote him. He didn't write back. End of story."

He swallowed a swig of his breakfast beer.

"That's the thing about being a writer, of course. Or being an editor. If you don't like the ending, you can always write a new one."

I took a swallow of my beer.

"Yeah. Or you can burn the book."

We finished our breakfasts, and I went upstairs to pack. I was going back to the land of Starbucks, malls, pink palaces, and bagels. I missed my father. I missed Lou, though I'd never tell him. I carried my bags downstairs.

Maria came toward me, clutching a rabbit. "This is José. I want you to take him with you."

"I couldn't," I stumbled, "I couldn't poss—"

"It would mean very much to me. To Mister Ri—to Roland. If you took him. To remember us."

"Trust me. Remembering the last two weeks will not be a problem."

"You shouldn't live alone. You should have someone." She stared at me earnestly, her black eyes making me uncomfortable.

"Maybe I should just take a bonsai."

"No. You should take the rabbit."

I nodded. I obviously wasn't leaving without the rabbit.

"I shouldn't live alone. Okay, so is the rabbit for company or protection? An attack rabbit?"

Maria looked at me quizzically. "José would never hurt anyone."

"Right."

Maria placed José in a travel case. Then she handed me a box full of rabbit food, carrots, and vegetables from the garden.

"Not too much lettuce. It will give him diarrhea."

"The last thing I want is a rabbit with the runs."

I took the rabbit and the box, and Roland grabbed my suitcase and laptop.

"I'll walk you to the car."

We made our way through the garden, past all of Maria's cats and orchids. I sensed the garden ghosts had been sent away.

"I really don't know how to thank you for teaching me to dance."

I shrugged. "José is more than enough, Roland."

"You'll like having his company."

"No…I won't."

"Well, thank you anyway. For everything. If I ever do write again, you'll be the first person I call."

Inwardly, I shuddered. Roland put José on the passenger side of my car, and I put my bags in the trunk.

"I'll be in touch," he said as he gave me another bear hug. I looked at him in the full light of day. Years of loss had been erased. He looked a decade younger than when I had arrived. As much as I wanted to hate him for not giving me a manuscript, for the deception of bringing me here in the first place, for writing a poem, not a novel, I couldn't.

"Don't forget to dance every night, Roland. You deserve a little happiness."

"I will. I'll dance. And maybe even write—"

"Don't say it." I shook my head. "I'll explain it to Lou somehow."

We hugged again, and I was on my way. Backward. Like the sun setting in the east now. Back to my world. All was the same, but maybe I wasn't.

29

My world kept spinning backward. After I arrived home, I drove to Stratford Oaks and visited my father. He hadn't missed me, because he hadn't remembered that I'd gone.

"Cassie..." He smiled and recognized me. He clutched my hand like a little boy clutching his mother as he learns to cross the street. Once my little hand fluttered like a baby bird inside of his. Now, he grasped at me, as if he knew he was falling away, out of the tree without knowing how to fly. Falling backward into a chasm that was deep and dark and permanent.

"Dad..." I pulled the ottoman closer to him and smiled, caressing his cheek. He coughed a great racking cough. I'd been told he had caught a bad cold. It came on suddenly. The doctor was due to see him on morning rounds.

"Damn cold. I need a tissue," he mumbled, though he

had a box of them on his lap. "Damn cold. Damn cold." He was being pulled away from me, and I fought to keep him.

"I'm sorry I haven't been here, Dad. I had to go see Roland Riggs. Remember? To help him with his book."

"Are you a writer?"

"No. An editor. But you know that, Dad."

His eyes were fading. And then, briefly, they focused.

"You have always made me very proud, Cassie. I love you. I love you truly." And then he coughed again. "Damn cold. Damn cold. Damn cold."

Eventually, he nodded off. I wrapped his legs in a blanket and kissed him on his forehead. I knew there would come a day, a moment, a line in the sand, after which he would never recognize me. The chasm would swallow him up, and I would stand on the edge. Utterly alone.

But that time never came. Two days later, he was transferred to Boca Community Hospital with pneumonia. He died two days after that.

I was there.

I wish I could say that we had another moment. A deathbed moment of recognition. But I consoled myself that we had what we had. A lifetime of closeness. He drifted off to sleep, and I held his hand while he took a last breath. One last deep, struggling breath. Then a groan. Then beeps and echoes of hospital machinery. Then nothing. I had signed a DNR order. He was gone.

Lou was there for the two days my father struggled to breathe in the hospital. We never spoke Roland's name. We didn't talk shop. We talked about my father and how he loved me. We talked about how my father had even tolerated my first husband, my last boyfriend, my temper, my rebelliousness.

"He saw himself in you, Cass," Lou said. "You're talented, but even if you were a shy, retiring housewife with a ditch-digging, beer-swilling husband and a minivan full of screaming brats, he would have loved you."

Even as Lou said it and I smiled at the ridiculousness of *me* being a housewife, I knew it was true. I was loved simply because I was born.

We cremated him. I didn't want an open-casket wake. I didn't want to look at a piece of waxen corpse and think of him in a box. So we cremated him. Just Lou and I were there beforehand. We didn't say prayers. Just words. "I miss you. I love you," I whispered before they took his body to be burned. For Lou, simply, "Say hello to Helen for me." I thought of scattering the ashes in the ocean. That seemed romantic to me. But my father hated the beach. Hated the sand and the stickiness and sweat. And after years of watching him slip away from me, I wanted him close. So I told them I wanted to take him home...to José and my apartment.

After they burned him, I returned to my apartment. It suddenly felt claustrophobic to me. Because now I had no other purpose. I would go to work; I would come home; I would drink coffee; I would drink tequila; I would stay up too late; but I would not now have Stratford Oaks. I wouldn't have somewhere to go and someone to love and care for. Maybe Maria was right. She needed her baby, Roland Riggs. My baby had died. Now I had no one. Only José.

Of course, I'd never had a pet my whole life, let alone a rabbit. But it was strange how José seemed to sense my grief. It washed over me like storm waves hitting the rocks on the beach, throwing me into the undertow until I could come up for a gasp of air, only to find myself swallowing my grief again like so much saltwater. José would hop over to my bed, which I refused to leave, and I would pick him up and let him sniff my shot glass of tequila, to which he'd shake his head back and forth and sort of sneeze. Then we'd watch TV, and José would come up to my face and nudge it.

After days of not answering my phone, and days of tequila and rabbit sniffles, I realized I was in sorry shape.

"José, with my track record in the romance department, I always assumed I would end up one of those batty old women with fifteen cats and a library card. Not that I ever would have a cat. But it's a cliché. Old lady with lots of cats. Kind of like 'fucks like a rabbit.' Cliché. However, and no offense to you, José, an old lady with a rabbit and a fifth of tequila by her bed watching re-runs of *Gilligan's Island* is far more pathetic. Old lady with a rabbit. It just sounds bad."

José took no offense.

Over the weekend, Roland called. I picked up the phone, though I had ignored Lou's calls for several days.

"Cassie?"

"Hmm?"

"I heard about your father from Lou. I'm very sorry. Very sorry. Grief can keep you a prisoner."

"You have a little experience in that department."

"Years and years I wasted, Cassie. Don't let it consume you. Go to London."

"London? I don't think so."

"Then go to Paris. Go to the moon. Just don't go where I went."

"I'll think about it, Roland."

"How's José?"

"About now? My best friend."

"That and a fifth of tequila, right?"

"We did get to know each other pretty well, didn't we?"

"Well...don't forget Maria and me. And Lou."

I found myself welling up. "I won't."

After I hung up the phone, I cried into José's fur. I missed my Daddy. Even if it meant just holding his hand and him never recognizing me again. Sometimes in life, you take what you can get. Sometimes what you can get isn't enough.

30

The cock that roared raised its proverbial head and called me. My ex-husband, the now semifamous rock star John Dillinger called late one evening. Assuming it was Lou, and knowing he'd hound me endlessly until I picked up the phone, I answered on the third ring.

"Cass, love?"

As if in a dream, I felt myself transported back to my early twenties, to that girl I used to be.

"Johnny?" I smiled, picturing his blond locks standing straight on end, which was how he used to wear them.

"I heard about your old man. Obit in the *New York Times,* sweetie. So sorry. Absolutely sucks like fuckin' eggs."

With poetry like that, how did I ever leave him?

"Thanks, Johnny."

"Are you okay?"

I stared at my bedside table of unwashed glasses with half-finished tequila at the bottom of each. José rested on my stomach, sleeping.

"Okay is a rather relative term in my life right now, Johnny. No…I would not say I am particularly okay," I sniffled. "I'm drinking like a fish and talking to a rabbit, which is far too complex to explain right now. But to answer your question, no. But it's not like you can do anything. Not like anyone can do anything."

"I know. Sometimes just knowin' someone cares though…you know. It can help. I could fly down and cheer you up. Take you down to South Beach and party and forget it all for a while."

I breathed deeply. Memories of his immense endowment flooded my mind. "No. I don't think that's a good idea. I'd sleep with you, you know. For old times' sake and all that. We never could resist each other. And I'm not sure that's a good idea."

"Couldn't hurt." I pictured his lopsided grin as he said it. Twice after our divorce, we ran into each other in Manhattan bars. Years apart did nothing to dim the sexual spark between us, and we raced home to my apartment both times and fucked. With us, it was never making love. It was five or six times a night, intense and fiercely physical. And when morning came, each time, I rolled over and thought what a mistake we made. He rolled over and grinned, but I knew he thought the same thing.

I laughed out loud. "Maybe… Maybe not, though. Can I ask you something?"

"Sure Cassie X. Sure," he said, calling me by my nickname, "X," from the little-known fact that my middle name is Xavria.

"Johnny, was I really a terrible wife?"

"Terrible? I don't know. You can't cook worth a fuck, you refuse to clean. You're moody, insensitive, drink too much, heaven help the man who speaks to you before you've had your coffee. You smoke too much—"

"I gave up smoking."

"Well, point one for Cassie X., then. No... you weren't a terrible wife. You always made me laugh. When you weren't hurling plates at me. And we were great in the sack, Cass. We always had that. Nothing quite compares."

"Come on. I read the gossip rags on occasion. I know you were rumored to have bedded two supermodels at the same time."

"I plead the fifth."

"There... see."

"But I didn't love them, Cass."

"I'm sorry I made such a mess of our marriage."

"Listen, Cass, we were just combustible, you know. Can't live with ya... can't live without ya. Mostly though...."

There was a long silence as he collected his thoughts, and I sensed he was going to chicken out of telling me whatever it was.

"You can tell me, Johnny."

"It was the time you had the flu. You know. That did it. That broke my heart."

There was another silence, and I tried hard to remember what the hell it was he was talking about.

The flu. It had hit me on a Friday. I tried to stay in the office, but Lou sent me home.

"For God's sake, Cassie, you look so frightening we had a copy editor quit this morning. Go home. Go home! You're white as a sheet."

I looked up from my desk. "Can't. Have to muddle through this latest book proposal from Lillian Palmer."

"No. It can wait. Go home. You'll get us all sick. And if I get the Hong Kong fucking flu, I promise you I will get even in ways you cannot in that young brain of yours yet imagine."

I tried feebly to grin. "Try me."

But in the end, I started feeling downright delirious. By the time my cab deposited me at Johnny's and my apartment building, I knew I was running a high fever. Upstairs, in my bathrobe, I took my temperature and watched it rocket to 104 degrees. I climbed into bed. I slept. I moaned. I whimpered. So now, I could not imagine what Johnny Dillinger was talking about. What the hell did that have to do with breaking his heart?

"Okay, Johnny. I remember the flu. I remember it was some sort of Asian flu. Some hellish flu that kept me in bed for four days, but what does that have to do with anything?"

"You wouldn't let me help you."

"What are you talking about?"

"Cassie, I have never cooked in my life. We ate takeout

constantly, but I went to the corner Korean grocer's and bought stuff to make soup. And I cooked and I...I tried to bring you compresses and aspirin and juice. And I made you soup, and you wouldn't eat it."

I took in what he said and felt a gnawing in my gut.

"You know," I finally said, quietly, "I have heard, all my life, that divorced people can boil down the reason for their divorce on a single straw that finally breaks the camel's back. The one thing that tips the scales and makes them realize the marriage is doomed. I can remember throwing plates at you, pulling a kitchen knife on you one time—"

"We were both drunk."

"Yes, but nonetheless, for most people that would be the defining moment. I cheated on you...one time, but...anyway, we rocked and rolled and tore each other apart and you remember that I didn't eat your soup?"

"It wasn't the soup. It was the act of making the soup. It was that I wanted to help you. I wanted, for once in our marriage, for you to *need* me. And you refused. You refused to need me. And I have written a hundred songs and sold lots of records because everyone, Cassie, needs to be needed, and when the person you love refuses to let down her guard, you can feel the cold and it ain't gonna work."

"Soup."

"Soup."

"I'm sorry, Johnny."

"You don't have to be sorry, Cassie. It was a long time ago."

"Well...if you were here now, I'd eat your soup."

"I'll fly there in a minute, Cass."

"I know. But I think we should maybe not do that, Johnny. It may have been about soup, but we really can't be together. We both know that."

"Sucks, don't it?"

"Like eggs, Johnny."

He was quiet, then whispered. "I liked your old man, Cass. He never judged me for all my tattoos and earrings."

"No. He didn't. He tried to love you. Even if he didn't understand us."

"Well, if you need anything, you call my management company in New York. They'll see I get the message."

"Thanks."

"Don't take this the wrong way, but I love you."

"Love you, too."

I hung up the phone and thought about Johnny's soup. It always came down to one moment. My father loved my mother for years after she left us. He just couldn't get over her. And then one Christmas—I was in the fourth grade—I was scheduled to be the Madonna in St. Mary's Holy Mother Catholic School's Annual Christmas Pageant. Though the nuns found me a bit on the unruly side, they were taken by my then-angelic face and naturally rosy cheeks.

Dressed in a white robe, I carried the baby brother of Margaret Foley to the manger, while Billy Collins played Joseph, even though he was shorter than I was. Seated on a bale of hay in the manger set up on stage, my father said he cried at how beautiful I was. Cameras snapped. Parents oohed and ahhed. My father looked around for my mother. She had pulled a no-show. Later she called and told him her dinner date had insisted they go for cocktails first. But it didn't matter what she said. She could have been in an ambulance with her legs amputated below the knees by a freak taxicab accident. In that one moment, as I played the mother of God, my father stopped loving my mother.

It was his soup.

"Soup," I said aloud to José. He looked at me, and his ears perked up. Finally, I picked up the telephone and dialed information.

"British Airways, please."

My palms felt clammy. But the gnawing feeling in my gut was giving way to butterflies. I had to know if Michael and I could be together or if we had already experienced our soup moment.

"I'd like information on flights to London from Miami."

31

I stared at my electronic ticket as it spat out from my printer. No turning back, I told myself even as my teeth chattered from nerves and lack of a decent meal since my father's death. I had the tequila shakes, and a long hot shower was in order. I stripped naked and started running the water. Then I heard a knock on my door.

"Fuck." I stopped the shower, threw on a robe and walked out to the living room to open my door.

"Hello, Lou," I said, unenthusiastically. But instead of Lou, I was staring at my mother.

"Mother? What the hell are you doing here?"

She was dressed in black, for mourning or fashion I had no idea. A Cartier watch flickered with diamonds on her wrist, and her blond highlights were freshly done. She reminded people of a famous French actress, and despite her age, she still turned heads.

"I'd invite you in, but I'm busy."

"I can see that by your bathrobe. Please, dahling," she murmured, "we need to talk."

"Fine," I said, tersely, and stepped aside. She click-clacked her way across the tile of my condo, her four-inch alligator pumps carrying her to my couch.

"I'm so very sorry about your father, Cassandra."

"I'm sure you are." I rolled my eyes and folded my arms. Somehow, she always brought out the fifteen-year-old in me.

"I am. I've been leaving messages for you like crazy at the office."

"They know better than to give them to me."

Her lips pursed in annoyance. "You've always been like this with me, Cassandra. Your father was always first in your life, and you never had room for me. Not even a tiny little bit."

I thought back to the missed school recitals and Saturday visits when she never showed. The time my father sent the housekeeper into my bedroom to talk to me about getting your first period and she awkwardly shoved a box of sanitary napkins at me while blushing and sweating. And I realized I was tired of fighting my mother. Tired of fighting life.

"I was never first in your life, Mother. I suppose it's payback."

"I left my marriage, not my child. But I could never

compete with the God who was your father. He was your Zeus atop Mount Olympus. Greater than mere mortals... and so I stayed away. I'm a former beauty queen, after all. I know competition. And if you know you can't win, there's no sense in playing."

I looked at my mother, this woman I barely knew but hated with all my being. It was all a fantasy. She had woven a tale so she could live with what she had done, which wasn't so different from the rest of us. What had I woven in my life to keep me away from Michael? That we could never be? That I could never love? Bedtime stories to get you through the long night. My mother was playing a game, and I had played it with her all these years.

"What do you want, Mother?"

"I remember being pregnant with you—"

"Please," I implored her. "Now isn't the time to wax poetic over your morning sickness."

"Indulge me, Cassandra. I remember it like it was yesterday. How thrilled we were to have this life growing inside of me, how very much in love we were. I know you think I don't mourn for him, but I do. It was a long time ago, but it was a part of me."

"I'm sure wherever he is—" I felt a thickening in my throat "—he appreciates that. So have we said all there is to say?"

"Not by a long shot. You've thought the worst of me. That all this time all I wanted was the percentage of the estate. That's such nonsense. I have all I could ever need or want."

"Five husbands will do that for you."

"For your information, I am married to my *fourth* husband, and I was widowed once. It's not so terrible."

"Anyway...you'll get your percentage after the lawyers probate."

"I don't want it. I'm giving it back to you. I suppose years ago, I thought you'd have children by now. So I had these grand images of putting the money in a trust and leaving my grandchild a small fortune. But at the rate you're going, Cassandra, I'll be long dead before you have a child."

"Thank you, Mother."

"Oh...I just mean that girls these days don't get married right after college. They take some time to figure out who they are and what they want. I wish I had done that."

"You did. You just had me first and *then* tried to figure out your life."

"I can see it was a waste of time to come here. I wanted you to know I am giving you back the money. I don't want it and never have. I came to tell you I am sorry he died. I am sorry I was not a perfect mother. I came to see if you might be interested in getting to know each other, but I can see you're not."

She stood up and smoothed her Chanel suit. She took a pair of Jackie O sunglasses from her purse and snapped the clasp of her Fendi handbag shut again with a perfect click. Perhaps that was why I hated her. Everything about her was so perfect. So concise. And I was so far from perfect. Everything about me from my hair to my bathroom to my love life was messy.

"It's too late, Mother. We've had our soup moment."

"Our what?"

"Our last straw."

"As long as I am still alive, I won't believe that. Maybe when you do have a child someday, if she's a daughter, you'll understand how complicated it can all be."

She click-clacked her way to the door and showed herself out. For a moment, I wanted to run after her. I wanted to be consoled and held by someone who once loved my father. I didn't want to be an orphan.

But the moment passed. I was alone.

32

"Spit?" Lou looked at me incredulously, as we sat in the front seat of his Jag. "You're trying to swallow that pill with spit?"

I nodded as the pill's bitterness seemed to spread across my tongue.

"Have you heard of this amazing new discovery called water?"

I swallowed. "Mmm-hmm. But we don't have any right now, and I felt like if I didn't take another Xanax this second I would puke."

"I know you know you're crazy so I will not point out the obvious."

I glanced at him out of the corner of my eye. "Appreciate it."

I had made my reservations to London with just two

days' notice and managed to pay an exorbitant sum of money for an otherwise empty transatlantic seat. Two days did not leave me much time to chicken out. I asked Lou to drive me to the airport because I planned on medicating myself into blindness. I hate to fly.

"Does Michael Pearton even know you're coming?"

I shook my head.

"So what if he's on vacation?"

"Then he'll have missed his chance."

"Just like that. The guy isn't home, and you say forget it?"

"It's either fate that we end up together or fate that we never meet."

"Fate."

"Yeah. God. Fate. Destiny."

"Since when did you start believing in fate?"

I thought of Roland Riggs and how his wife had been killed by a gunshot. I thought of Maria and how she had been brought to a tiny island by a bastard of a husband— who happened to like to fish. For empty years she and Roland walked among the living but were really dead. And in that house, thanks to a dose of disco, a Pulitzer winner had wooed his ladylove. They found each other. Fate.

"I don't know. I just do. Now. It's all too complicated to explain, and my head is getting fuzzy. I think I need another Xanax."

"How many have you taken?" Lou asked.

"Five."

"Christ almighty, Cassie, that's enough to put down a horse."

"I'm a thoroughbred, and I'm not down yet."

Lou reached across the creamy-beige soft leather seats and squeezed my hand.

"When you get to London, Cassie, I think he's going to be there. And I think if you would let it happen the way it's supposed to, then maybe it will all fall into place."

I looked Lou in the eyes. "Or I could fucking hate him. I could look at the way he folds the newspaper after breakfast in the morning and decide he's entirely too anal-retentive and be filled with loathing for him. Relationships happen that way, you know."

"*Your* relationships happen that way. Look at me and Helen, God rest her soul."

"Well, there you go."

"What?"

"You can fall in love and be together forever and then the person dies on you. They leave you in the end, one way or the other."

Lou was still holding my hand. He took it away and moved it to my face, pushing back a curl from my right eye. "Cassie," he whispered, "it isn't your mother you're mad at. It's *life* you're angry at. People leave. Period. They move on; they get sick; they die. That's life, darling. That's life. But if you let that stop you from living, then what's the point of it all?"

I looked at him until I couldn't anymore because I thought I might cry. I moved away from him and stared down at my watch, trying to focus on the numbers, which seemed to be swimming.

"I need a drink before I get on that plane."

"It's 11:00 a.m."

"It's happy hour in London."

He sighed. "All right then, let's go buy you a cocktail. I pray to God you land in London alive."

"Tell that to my pilot."

Lou popped open the trunk of his car and took out my lone suitcase. A small one with enough clothes for four days. I figured I didn't want to push my luck by staying too long that I might get sick of Michael just for the sake of getting sick of him.

We walked a long way to the terminal and sought out a bar.

"Tequila. Up, in a shot glass," I muttered to the bartender, a flat-nosed guy with a pock-marked face who looked like he'd been beat up a few times too many. The noise and hubbub of the airport was making my head feel like I was underwater. That and the Xanax. I receded into myself, falling into the warm ocean of Florida in August and letting the saltwater keep me buoyant. I tossed back my tequila, slammed down the shot glass, and made my way to the security checkpoint, Lou at my side with my carry-on.

On the line for security, Lou faced me, my bag on the floor between us. "Without Roland's book, we're in deep dog-shit this coming season. But don't feel any pressure to get Michael to finish his book or anything."

"I won't." I smiled at him. My teeth were buzzing.

"Be careful. Tell the stewardess to poke you every once in a while to make sure you're still breathing."

"Sure thing, Lou," I said from somewhere under the water. I thought I saw a mermaid swim by. A mermaid who looked like my mother. Hallucinations. Now I was having hallucinations. Just what I needed pre-flight.

Lou pulled me close. "I love you, Cass. Now get the fuck out of here. Leave the country already."

I allowed him to envelop me, and I enjoyed his scent. An old-man scent, sort of like my father's. Aqua Velva... and I even thought I smelled the dry-cleaning chemicals on his shirt. From an underwater canyon, I heard myself whisper, "I love you, too." When the words left my lips, I wondered who had said them.

Lou stepped away from me and smiled. Then, wiping his eyes, he headed up the ramp and back into the main terminal.

When I could no longer see him in the crowd, I went through the metal detector and then down to my gate to check in at the desk. I had asked for an aisle seat in first class. I felt my breathing grow heavier as I talked to the counter agent.

"We'll be boarding in an hour and fifteen minutes. We're scheduled to leave on time."

"Nearest pay phone?"

"Right over there, past the bathrooms, there's a bank of them."

"Thanks." I smiled back and headed over to the phones. Taking out my calling card, I dialed my mother.

"Hello?" A woman's accented voice answered the phone.

"Is Sophia there, please?"

"May I tell her who's calling?"

"Cassie Hayes."

My mother's maid put the telephone down, and I heard an assortment of footsteps and clicking heels on marble.

"Cassandra?"

"Hello, Sophia."

"I've been thinking about our visit."

"It was too short to call a visit, Mother."

"See…there you go again. Is it so hard to be nice to me?"

"Yes."

She was silent. After a long sigh, she said, softly, "I know you don't believe this, but I really do want to be a part of your life."

I wanted, almost more than anything, to say, "Well, then where were you all these years?" But I heard Lou's voice. What was I really angry at? I heard my own breath, like a diver listening to the regulator. Breathe in. Breathe in. The mermaid floated by again, looking at me. I said, instead, "Don't you think it's too late?"

"Never. It's never too late. Where are you calling me from?"

"The airport. I'm leaving for London, and I just, inexplicably, wanted to say goodbye. In case the plane crashes."

"Heavens no. It won't, dear. Don't you know flying is safer than driving? Stan and I fly all the time. He has a Gulfstream, you know."

"Fascinating."

"When will you be back?"

"Not sure. But I'll call you. Maybe we can have dinner."

Her voice grew tremulous. "I would really like that, Cassandra. I really would." She sounded happy. "Ha-have a good trip. A safe trip. Be...careful."

"Okay. I'll call you, Sophia."

I hung up. The mermaid was gone. She had floated away. I had let her go. Tossed back to Copenhagen.

I picked up the phone again and placed a call to Michael.

"Hello?"

"Fuck you, Michael. You've avoided my calls and won't return e-mails. I was hoping you'd been in a car accident so you'd have a good excuse."

I heard him inhale. "Cassie?"

"Yes, of course it's me. Who else would open with 'fuck you'?"

"Oh, regularly my dear old sainted mother calls me and says, 'Fuck you, son.' But she calls me 'son,' not Michael, so I suppose that's how I will tell you apart."

I smiled despite feeling water rush by me in a torrent. I needed another drink.

"You're mother's dead, so you're lying. Doesn't matter. I'm coming to see you."

"Sure you are." At that moment, a voice over the P.A. system called out a flight number.

"What was that?"

"What?"

"That voice."

"I'm at the airport."

"You are not."

"Don't believe me. I'll be at your place by tomorrow morning, and if you haven't cooked me breakfast, I will turn around and come home."

"Shit."

"Shit? Fine, you don't want me to come, Michael."

"No, you bloody, stupid girl. I'm just not ready. You can't."

"Well, it's too God damn late, Michael. I'll see you tomorrow."

I hung up the phone before he could respond and walked back over to my gate. I kept hearing my breath and thought maybe Lou was right. Maybe I should make them poke me to check my coma status every once in a while.

I sat and waited until they called my flight. I reminded myself to breathe. Breathe like a diver. Take in the air in my tank. The plane will not crash. The plane will not crash. And Michael and I just might not hate each other.

The possibilities were staggering. At least they seemed that way after a tequila and five tranquilizers. I rose unsteadily on my feet and headed toward the plane.

33

"Miss?...Miss?"

From the fuzzy recesses of my brain, I was aware of two things: someone was poking me...harder by the minute, and I was drooling.

"Hmm?" I sat up, my head throbbing, and wiped the corner of my mouth.

"Hot towel?"

"No. I really just want to sleep my way to London. That way, I don't have to think about crashing."

The flight attendant, a frosty blonde with a neat chignon, pale English skin and rose-colored lipstick looked worried. Her nametag read "Claire."

"You mustn't worry about crashing."

"Yeah, well I'm going to every waking minute. So that's

why I don't want to be woken up until we get to London."

"Would you like a pillow?"

"Sure."

While Claire went to find me one, I stared at the phone in front of me. Through the miracle of modern technology, I could talk to Michael mid-flight. What did "I'm not ready" mean?

I plugged my credit card into the phone and dialed.

"Fuck you. What the hell does 'I'm not ready' mean?"

"Mother? I'm sorry, but Cassie is finally coming to see me and I don't have time to chit-chat."

"I mean it, Michael. I will turn around and fly back to Florida. This was your idea, and now I'm coming and you tell me you're not ready?"

"I just meant that I will have to stay up half the night cleaning and getting this place in order and grocery shopping for coffee and ordering you fresh roses. I'll send my driver to pick you up. What's your flight number?"

"Your driver. That's so... I don't know. So English."

"Your flight, Cassie," he demanded.

I gave it to him and heard how nervous he sounded.

I said, "Now you're not sure, are you? If we should meet. I told you I don't screw on the toothpaste cap and I don't pick up after myself, and I drink too much and eat too little. Terrible food. Loaded with MSG. Takeout. And there you were, Michael, blithely ignorant. Telling me it would all be wonderful if we could just meet. We were destined to be together. And now you don't know because it's all about to become reality. It's that way with fantasy, dear. Prepare to be disillusioned. I *am* as terrible as I say I am."

"And I am not everything that I have said I am. But it is too late for me to fix that. I just promise to explain it all."

"Explain what all."

"It's complicated."

"You're married, aren't you?"

"No."

"You have seven bratty children."

"No."

"You have a ghostwriter and are not the brilliant author I think you are."

"No. Just get here, Cassie. Get here so I can touch you."

I felt myself grow wet thinking of it. I felt my knees briefly weaken and was grateful I was sitting down.

"I have to go. Claire is bringing me a pillow."

"Claire?"

"My flight attendant. But don't think this is beauty rest. I assure you I will look terrible tomorrow. Hungover and red-eyed and skin all dry and hair a fright."

"Sounds charming. I'll make eggs."

"See you, then."

"Yes, see you."

I hung up and fell into the dark, empty dreamless sleep of drugs and alcohol. I was tired of thinking about Michael. I welcomed the blackness as it descended upon me like a heavy blanket.

34

Claire, with her perfectly clipped English accent, was trying to rouse me. I landed back to earth from the blackness of my drug-induced night with a thud.

"We're here."

"Where?"

"Heathrow. We've landed. Everyone else has deplaned."

"Oh." I tried to think but my temples were beating the inside of my brain. "I've changed my mind. Take me back to Miami."

"We can't do that. You'd have to make new reservations and...you are kidding, right?"

I pitied the perfectly orderly Claire and pulled myself together. "No. I'm not, but I will get off your plane. This plane, which you so magnificently landed in London."

Staring at me as one perhaps stares at Great Aunt

Gertrude when she does her amazing "turn the eyelids inside-out trick" at the family reunion, the stewardess helped me gather my things and leave the plane.

My first order of business was to get a bit of the hair of the dog that bit me. Then take a Percocet for my world-class headache. I searched the near-empty terminal for a bar, and instead spotted a well-dressed man in a chauffeur's cap waiting patiently by my gate. He waved at me and started walking briskly in my direction.

"Miss Hayes, so glad you could make it."

"And you would be?"

"Charles...Charlie. I'm Mr. Pearton's driver...and cook and chief bottle-washer."

"Well, I look a fright, and my head is killing me. And I just don't think I'm ready to see Mr. Pearton."

"Well, we have an hour's drive. There's champagne waiting in the car, and you can freshen up in the ladies' room. I'll wait."

"I don't think you understand. I can't believe I've flown over here on a night's notice. Normal people don't do things like this. Not that I'm normal. But I really don't think this is the way Michael and I should meet."

"Well, I for one, ma'am, have been waiting six long years for you to come to London. I have listened to him talk about you. I know what he goes through when he writes. I know he can't write without you. So you see, I've waited quite long enough, and I'm prepared to wait until noon for you to freshen up. The loo is over there."

I stared at Charlie. He was ageless. An old man who had

long since stopped aging and was simply well-preserved. His hair was trimmed, his hands neatly manicured. He had a few wrinkles near his eyes, and his skin was liver-spotted but pink and rosy by his cheeks. His blue eyes twinkled, and I knew, without a doubt, that he would indeed wait forever but I was *going* to meet his employer.

In the brightly lit ladies' room, I looked positively sick. My skin was pale and pasty. I stuck my tongue out at my reflection. White…chalky. I sighed and took out my makeup bag. I brushed my teeth, spitting into the sink of the British Airways terminal bathroom, silver and gleaming, and now full of my toothpaste. My hair was beyond help, so I merely pushed and poked it so all the matted curls wouldn't be in the one lone place I had smashed my head against the seat. I applied fresh makeup, smoothed my sweater, and went out to face Charles and customs.

Michael's car was a Bentley. "How English of him." I smiled at Charles.

"She's a dream to drive."

I climbed into the back seat and put my carry-on next to me. Charles sat in the front seat—on the "wrong" side, of course—and we were off, pulling through the quiet streets of early-morning London, foggy with a slight drizzle.

Charles kept looking at me in the rearview mirror. I felt my curly hair growing frizzier by each damp second I was in England. Frizzier, for me, is not a good look.

"I know." I smiled at Charles. "You're thinking 'All this excitement for her?' A shower will help me immensely, I assure you."

"I wasn't thinking that at all. I was thinking how happy he is going to be to see you finally. It will do him a world of good."

"A world of good? Why? Does he have writer's block again?"

"I can't say, ma'am. I can't say. But it will do him good. Very good."

Michael Pearton's writer's blocks were legend around the office. Not only did I have to talk with him for hours on the phone to nurse him out of it, we all had to hold our breath. More than once we had already planned out a cover and jacket only to discover he had trashed his original ideas and gone off in another direction—A.B. Our codes were B.B.—Before Block—and A.B. for After Block.

Charles kept glancing at me in the rearview mirror, a worried expression on his face. "You really don't know, do you, ma'am?"

"I really don't, but you're scaring me."

"I'm just glad you came...for his sake."

"Charlie, I needed to come for my sake."

I half-dozed and before I knew it we were pulling up a long, somewhat bumpy drive to an English country manor.

"I had no idea he lived in such a majestic house."

"It's been in the family forever. A bit drafty but lovely, Miss Hayes. You should see it when the gardens bloom."

Charles parked the car. I heard him inhale deeply as he opened my door.

"Are you nervous, Charlie?" I glanced at him.

"Just a bit, Miss Hayes."

"Well, if I'm going to call you Charlie, you have to call me Cassie. And we'll all know shortly whether this is a huge mistake, won't we?"

He led me up the steps and into a large foyer.

"I'll put your bags in your room. He's waiting for you in his study. That door over there."

Hoping my knees wouldn't fail me, and surprised I had forgotten my headache in all the anticipation, I walked over to Michael Pearton's door and opened it.

35

In the grayness of the London morning, the study was dimly lit with a small lamp on a desk. A fire filled the room with the scent of pine.

"Cassie." Michael smiled at me, and I felt my breath rush out of me. It was as if my soul left my body and traveled somewhere to be pieced together whole again. It landed back in my body with a force like the hammering of my heart, and I knew I was whole.

But he was not. Michael Pearton smiled at me from a wheelchair.

I walked to him and knelt down, my knees shaking from fear.

"What's this?"

"A wheelchair."

"Don't be an ass. What's it for? I don't understand."

"First kiss me. Because if you tell me you're headed back to Florida tomorrow, I want to have at least kissed you."

He pulled me into his lap, and I wrapped my arms around his neck. He pressed his hands against the small of my back, as if to will us to be one. We kissed for a long time without breathing. Or maybe we breathed each other. And when we finally stopped to look at each other again, I saw his face was as beautiful as in all his pictures. I almost forgot for a moment that the man I had waited all these years to meet was in a chrome-wheeled chair.

"Want to know something funny, Cassie?" he asked, stroking my hair.

"My hair? The weather does nothing for it."

"No…it's just that four days ago, I was walking. Tripping a lot, but walking. I've got M.S., Cassie. And then when you phoned and said you were coming, I had to clean in record time, and I wanted to have the place not look like a bloody old dark English castle. And I overdid it, and here I am in this stupid thing."

"M.S. Oh, Michael…I'm so sorry."

His eyes clouded briefly. "Don't be, Cassie. I do okay usually. I don't plan on dying on you or anything like that. But I realize it stacks the whole pile of cards against us. Against you. We can have this weekend, and after that you can leave, and I'll understand, Cassie."

"Michael, if there's one thing by now you must know, it's that I am a terrible bitch. And if you think this elaborate ploy to get rid of me is going to work, you're fucking crazy." I traced my finger down the scar on his face. I imagined waking up to that scar and to all of him for a very long time.

"I knew I could count on you to stay with me for sympathy reasons."

"Not on your life. I want breakfast. And I'll tell you right now I don't do dishes."

"Let me guess, you break them when you're through."

"I've been known to on occasion."

"And after breakfast?" He raised an eyebrow.

"I'm going to fuck your brains out. And then we'll read the paper in bed. And then we'll have soup for lunch."

"Soup?"

I smiled. "Yes."

"And how do you want your eggs, Cassie?"

"Didn't this all start with eggs?"

"What?"

"Your last session of writer's block."

"I believe it did."

"For once, I'll have blind trust, Michael. Make them any way you bloody want."

"A girl after my own heart."

I stood up and walked behind his wheelchair.

"I can wheel myself, Cassie. It's all right. I feel so stupid ending up in this thing when here you've flown from America."

"I'll push. Take it as a sign of my undying devotion."

"My nurse?"

"No. I'll take it out in trade later."

"You are a naughty girl."

"That's what they tell me, Michael. That's what they tell me."

I pushed Michael out into the hallway. Charlie hadn't moved. He was standing as I'd left him beside my bags.

"She's here to stay, Charlie."

"For how long?" Charlie asked.

Instinctively, I found myself gripping Michael's shoulder. Why had it taken me so long to realize?

"Long enough to call this place home."

36

Dear Lou,

Another rainy day. I can almost not stand it. No wonder the British lost the Revolutionary War. They were all clinically depressed. I miss the Florida sun.

Michael is walking again, and we're doing unbelievably well. Happy. Just happy, Lou. Except for the rain.

How is my rabbit? Give José a kiss for me and then give yourself a kiss. And then, get ready to want to kiss me back and do a jig.

Enclosed please find the sequel to *Simple Simon*.

Roland Riggs had it all along. He had written it after his wife died and kept it all these years. It's full of the raw emotion only love and death can bring to writing. It's brilliant. You will be wealthy beyond your wildest dreams. Roland told me he had to be sure I was the right person for the book. Now that I am here with Michael, I am that person.

Roland and Maria got married just three weeks after I left. You asked me if I now believe in fate. I do. And Maria is pregnant. Now I also believe in miracles.

In your last e-mail you wondered when I will return. I can't say. Michael and I will probably come for several months. Go back and forth between my home and his. But even though the weather is a bitch on my hair, and I can't say I haven't thrown any plates or threatened to kill him, he is, was always, and forever will be, my true north.

In Roland's book, Simon falls in love, but the war follows him home. Death is everywhere. It's in his morning coffee; it lingers on his toothbrush. Roland was ready to let go and believe in love again. He rewrote the ending. Simon is healed.

So am I.

I will call you when Michael and I are coming.

Eternally Yours,

Cassie

P.S. Don't think because I fell in love that you all can get away with ruining this manuscript. I've edited it, and if you or Troy change a single word of it, I'll have your testicles.

Book Group Questions

1. Many of Cassie's fears revolve around losing control. How has the author woven this theme throughout the book?

2. Cassie's ex says people who are in love need to be needed. Do you think this is true? What does the "soup moment" say about Cassie?

3. How do the themes of life and death permeate the book?

4. Disco and tango are discussed in the book, or are danced by the characters. Why disco?

5. Cassie's ex is called the "cock that roared." That relationship is sexual but not cerebral. Michael Pearton and Cassie have never met. Their relationship is cerebral, not sexual. Which is more powerful? Can you love someone you've never met?

6. How do each of the main characters grieve?

7. What do you think the author is saying about celebrity culture?

8. Were you surprised at Michael Pearton in the end? Why do you think the author chose to present him this way?

Out of the Blue

Isabel Wolff

This book is for every woman who has let a breeze of doubt turn into a full-blown hurricane!

Faith Martin, AM-U.K.!'s face of the morning weather, is used to delivering the forecast, not being told the forecast—especially when it concerns her marriage.

When Faith's ultraglam best friend plants a seed of doubt about her husband's fidelity, she begins to question everything about her comfortable life.

"Wolff handles the breakdown of marriage with warmth and humor."
—*The Times*

Name & Address Withheld

Jane Sigaloff

Life couldn't be better for Lizzie Ford. Not only
does she have a great job doling out advice on the
radio, but now she has a new love interest *and* a
new best friend. Unfortunately she's about to learn
that they're husband and wife. Can this expert on
social etiquette keep the man, her friend *and* her
principles? Find out in *Name & Address Withheld,*
a bittersweet comedy of morals and manners.

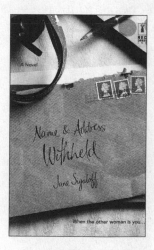